Dear Reader,

Christmas is coming up, and I'm going to get stuck with my friend Ada's horrible brother, Egan, for the duration. We don't get along. Egan thinks I'm a female Don Juan because I write racy novels, and I think he's the ranching community's answer to Frankenstein's monster. We argue about everything. I live in New York City and write historical romances. He's a rancher from Wyoming with a degree in political science. We're total opposites. But I have to admit, when the light's just right and he isn't being a royal pain in the neck, he's very, very attractive. I'm glad he doesn't know. If he ever realized how I really felt about him, who knows what might happen...?

Kati James

Please address questions and book requests to: Silhouette Reader Service
U.S.: 3010 Walden Ave., P.O. Box 1325, Buffalo, NY 14269
Canadian: P.O. Box 609, Fort Erie, Ont. L2A 5X3

DIANA PALMER

HEART OF ICE

Silhouette Books

Published by Silhouette Books

America's Publisher of Contemporary Romance

SILHOUETTE BOOKS
300 East 42nd St.,
New York, N.Y. 10017

ISBN 0-373-88524-5

HEART OF ICE

Chapter One

"**Y**ou didn't!" Katriane wailed at her best friend. "Not at Christmas!"

Ada looked pained and visibly shrank an inch. "Now, Kati..." she began placatingly, using the nickname she'd given the taller girl years ago. "It's a huge apartment. Absolutely huge. And you and I will be going to parties all over town, and there's the charity ball at the Thomsons'... It will be all right, you'll see. You won't even notice that he's here."

"I'll notice," Kati said shortly. Her reddish gold hair blazed in the ceiling light, and her brown eyes glared.

"It's our first Christmas without Mother," Ada tried again. "He's got nobody but me."

"You could go to the ranch for Christmas," Kati suggested, hating the idea even as she said it.

"And leave you here alone? What kind of friend would I be then?"

"The kind who isn't sticking me with her horrible brother during my one holiday a year!" came the hot reply. "I worked myself to the bone, researching that last book. I was taking a rest between contractual obligations...just Christmas. How can I rest with Egan here!"

"He'll be fun to have around," Ada suggested softly.

"We'll kill each other!" Kati groaned. "Ada, why do you hate me? You know Egan and I don't get along. We've never gotten along. For heaven's sake, I can't live under the same roof with your brother until

Christmas! Have you forgotten what happened last time?''

Ada cleared her throat. "Look, you planned to set that next big historical in Wyoming, didn't you, on a ranch? Who knows more about ranching in Wyoming than Egan? You could look upon it as an educational experience—research.''

Kati just glared.

"Deep down,'' Ada observed, "you both probably really like each other. It's just that you can't... admit it.''

"Deep down,'' her friend replied, "I hate him. Hate. As in to dislike intensely. As in to obsessively dislike.''

"That's splitting an infinitive,'' Ada pointed out.

"You are an actress, not an educator,'' came the sharp retort.

Ada sighed, looking small and dark and vulnerable. So unlike her elder brother. "I may wind up being an educator, at this rate,'' she said. "I am sort of between jobs.''

"You'll get another one," Kati said easily. "I've never seen anyone with your talent. You got rave reviews in your last play."

"Well, maybe something will turn up. But, getting back to Egan . . ."

"Must we?" Kati groaned. She turned, worrying the thick waves of her long hair irritatedly. "Don't do this to me, Ada. Uninvite him."

"I can't. He's already on the way."

"Now?" Kati looked hunted. She threw up her hands. "First my royalty check gets lost in the mail when my car payment is due. Now I wind up with a sidewinder to spend Christmas with. . . ."

"He's my brother," Ada said in a small voice. "He has no one. Not even a girl friend."

"Egan?" Two eyebrows went straight up. "Egan always has a girl friend. He's never between women."

"He is right now."

"Did he go broke?" Kati asked with a sweet smile.

"Now, Kati, he's not that bad to look at."

That was true enough. Egan had a body most men would envy. But his face was definitely not handsome. It was craggy and rough and uncompromising. Just like Egan. She could see those glittering silver eyes in her sleep sometimes, haunting her, accusing her—the way they had that last time. She hated Egan because he'd misjudged her so terribly. And because he'd never admitted it. Not then, or since.

She folded her arms over her breasts with a curt sigh. "Well, Mary Savage used to think he was Mr. America," she conceded.

Ada eyed her closely. "He's just a poor, lonely old cattleman. He can't help it if women fall all over him."

"Egan Winthrop, poor? Lonely?" Kati pursed her lips. "The old part sounds about right, though."

"He's thirty-four," Ada reminded her. "Hardly in his dotage."

"Sounds ancient to me," Kati murmured, staring out over the jeweled night skyline of Manhattan.

"We're both twenty-five." Ada laughed. "Nine years isn't so much."

"Fudge." She leaned her head against the cold windowpane. "He hates me, Ada," she said after a minute, and felt the chill all up and down her body. "He'll start a fight as sure as there's a sun in the sky. He always starts something."

"Yes, I know," Ada confessed. She joined the taller woman at the window. "I don't understand why you set him off. He's usually the soul of chivalry with women."

"I've seen him in action," Kati said quietly. "You don't have to tell me about that silky charm. But it's all surface, Ada. Egan lets nobody close enough to wound."

"For someone who's been around him only a few times in recent years, and under the greatest pressure from me, you seem to know him awfully well," Ada mumbled.

"I know his type," she said shortly. "He's a taker, not a giver."

"Neither one of you ever gives an inch," Ada remarked. She studied her friend closely. "But I had to invite him. He's the only family I have."

Kati sighed, feeling oddly guilty. She hugged the shorter girl impulsively. "I'm sorry. I'm being ratty and I don't mean to. You're my friend. Of course you can invite your awful brother for Christmas. I'll grit my teeth and go dancing with Jack and pretend I love having him here. Okay?"

"That I'll have to see to believe."

Kati crossed her heart. "Honest."

"Well, since that's settled, how about if we go and get a Christmas tree?" Ada suggested brightly.

Kati laughed. "Super," she said and grabbed up her coat to follow Ada out the door. "And if we get one big enough," she mumbled under her breath, "maybe we can hang Egan from one of the limbs."

They trudged through four tree lots before they found just the right tree. It was a six-foot Scotch pine, full and bushy and perfect for their apartment. They stuffed it into the back of Kati's Thunderbird and carried it home, along with boxes of ornaments and new tinsel to add to their three-year supply in the closet.

Ada went out to get a pizza while Kati tied ribbon through the bright balls and hung them lovingly on the tree. She turned on some Christmas music and tried not to think about Egan. It seemed so long ago that they'd had that horrible blowup....

It had been five years since Kati first set eyes on Egan Winthrop. She and Ada had met at school, where both were majoring in education. Ada had later switched to drama, and Kati had decided to study English while she broke into the fiction market in a small way. Three years ago, after graduation, they'd taken this apartment together.

Egan and Kati had been at odds almost from the first. Kati got her first glimpse of the tall rancher at school, when she and Ada were named to the college honors society in their junior year. Egan and Mrs. Winthrop had both come. Kati had no relatives, and Ada had quickly included her in family plans for an evening out afterward. Egan hadn't liked that. From the first meeting of eyes, it had been war. He disapproved vehemently of Kati's chosen profession, although he was careful not to let Ada or his mother see just how much he disliked Kati. They'd hardly spoken two words until that fateful summer when Kati had flown out to the ranch with Ada for the Fourth of July.

It had been the first year she'd roomed with Ada, almost three years ago. Ada's mother had been diagnosed with cancer, and the family knew that despite the treatments, it would only be a matter of a year or two before she wouldn't be with them. Everyone had gone to the Wyoming ranch for the July Fourth holidays—including Kati, because Ada refused to leave her alone in New York. Kati's parents were middle-aged when she was born, and had died only a little apart just before she finished high school. She had cousins and uncles and aunts, but none of them would miss her during the July vacation. So, dreading Egan's company, she'd put on a happy face and gone.

She couldn't forget Egan's face when he'd seen her getting off the plane with his sister.

He hadn't even bothered to disguise his distaste. Egan had a mistaken view of romance writers' morals and assumed that Kati lived the wild life of her heroines. It wasn't true, but it seemed to suit him to believe that it was. He gave her a chilly reception, his silvery eyes telling her that he wished she'd stayed in New York.

But his cousin Richard's enthusiastic greeting more than made up for Egan's rudeness. She was hugged and hugged and enthused over, and she ate it up. Richard was just her age, a dark-haired, dark-eyed architect with a bright future and a way with women. If he hadn't been such a delightful flirt, the whole incident might have been avoided. But he had been, and it wasn't.

Richard had taken Kati to the Grand Teton National Park for the day, while Mrs. Winthrop soaked up the attention she was getting from her son and daughter. She was a lot like Ada, a happy, well-adjusted person with a loving disposition. And none of Egan's cynicism. Kati had liked her very much. But she and Richard had felt that

Mrs. Winthrop needed some time alone with her children. So they'd driven to the park and hiked and enjoyed the beauty of the mountains rising starkly from the valley, and afterward they'd stopped in Jackson for steaks and a salad.

On the way home, Richard's car had had a flat tire. Richard, being the lovable feather-brain he was, had no spare. In that part of the country on a holiday night, there wasn't a lot of traffic. So they walked back to the ranch—which took until four in the morning.

Egan had been waiting up. He said nothing to Richard, who was so tired that he was hardly able to stand. Richard went inside, leaving all the explanations to Kati.

"You live down to your reputation, don't you?" he asked with a smile that chilled even in memory. "My God, you might have had a little consideration for my mother. She worried."

Kati remembered trying to speak, but he cut her off with a rough curse.

"Don't make it worse by lying," he growled. "We both know what you are... you with your loose morals and your disgusting books. What you do with my cousin is your business, but I don't want my holidays ruined by someone like you. You're not welcome here any longer. Make some excuse to leave tomorrow."

And he walked away, leaving Kati sick and near tears. She hadn't let them show, she was too proud. And she'd managed to get to bed without waking Ada, who shared a room with her. But the next morning, cold-eyed and hating Egan more than ever, she packed her suitcase, gave some excuse about an unexpected deadline and asked Richard to take her to the airport.

They were on the porch when Egan came out the front door, looking irritated and angry and strangely haggard.

"I'd like to speak to you," he told Kati.

She remembered looking at him as if he were some form of bacteria, her back stiff, her eyes full of hatred.

"Go ahead," she told him.

He glared at Richard, who cleared his throat and mumbled something about getting the car.

"Why didn't you tell me what happened?" he asked.

"Why bother, when you already knew?" she asked in glacial tones.

"I didn't know," he ground out.

"How amazing," she replied calmly. "I thought you knew everything. You seem to have made a hobby out of my life—the fictionalized version, of course."

He looked uncomfortable, but he didn't apologize. "Richard had been drinking. It was four in the morning—"

"We had a very long walk," she told him curtly. "About fifteen or twenty miles. Richard wasn't drunk; he was tired." Her dark eyes glittered up at him. "I didn't like you much before, Mr. Winthrop, but I like you even less now. I'll make a point of keeping out of your vicinity. I wouldn't want to contaminate you."

"Miss James . . ." he began quietly.

"Good-bye." She brushed past him, suit-case in hand, and got into Richard's car. Ada and Mrs. Winthrop had tried to talk her into staying, but she was adamant about having an unexpected deadline and work pressure. And to this day, only she and that animal in Wyoming really knew why she'd left. Even Richard hadn't been privy to the truth.

That episode had brought the antagonism between Egan and Kati out into the open, and their relationship seemed to go from bad to worse. It was impossible for Kati to stay in the same room with Egan these days. He'd find an excuse, any excuse, to nick her temper. And she'd always retaliate. Like last year...

Egan had been in town for some kind of conference and had stopped by the apart-ment to see Ada. Kati had been on her way to a department store in downtown Man-hattan to autograph copies of her latest book, *Renegade Lover,* a historical set in eighteenth-century South Carolina. Egan had walked in to find her in her autograph-ing clothes—a burgundy velvet dress cut low in front, and a matching burgundy hat crowned by white feathers. She'd looked like the heroine on the front of her book, and he immediately pounced.

"My God, Madame Pompadour," he observed, studying her from his superior height.

She bristled, glaring up at him. "Wrong country," she replied. "But I wouldn't expect you to know that."

His eyebrow jerked. "Why not? Just because I'm in oil and cattle doesn't make me an ignoramus."

"I never said a word, Mr. Winthrop, honey," she replied, batting her long eyelashes at him.

The term of endearment, on reflection, must have been what set him off. His lips curled in an unpleasant smile. "You do look the part, all right," he replied. "You could stand on the street corner and make a nice little nest egg . . ."

She actually slapped him—and didn't even realize she had until she felt her fingers stinging and saw the red mark along his cheek.

"Damn you!" she breathed, shaking with fury.

His nostrils flared; his eyes narrowed and became frankly dangerous. "Lift your hand to me again, ever," he said in that low, cold tone, "and you'll wish you'd never set eyes on me."

"I already do, Egan Almighty Winthrop! I already do."

"Dress like a tramp and people are going to label you one," he rejoined. His eyes cut away from her with distaste. "I wouldn't be seen in public with you."

"Thank God!" she threw after him, almost jumping up and down with indignation. "I wouldn't want people to think I cared so little about who I was seen with!"

At that moment, luckily, Ada had rushed in from her bedroom to play peacemaker. Without another word, Kati had grabbed up her coat and purse and had run from the apartment, tears rolling down her cheeks. It was a miracle that she managed to get herself back together by the time she reached the department store.

That was the last time she'd seen Egan Winthrop. And she never wanted to see him again. Oh, why had Ada agreed to let him come, knowing the state of hostility that existed between Egan and her? Why!

She put the last ball on the tree, and was reaching for the little golden angel that would sit atop it when she heard the door open.

It must be Ada with the pizza, of course, and she was starved. She reached up, slender in jeans and a pullover yellow velour sweater, laughing as she put the angel in place. As she moved, she knocked into one of the balls, but caught it just in time to keep it from dropping to the carpet.

"Back already?" she called. "I'm starved to death! Do you want to have it in here by the tree?"

There was a pregnant pause, and she felt eyes watching her. Nervous, she turned—to find herself staring at Egan Winthrop. Her hand clenched at the sight of him—so powerful and dark in his gray vested suit—and the fragile ball shattered under the pressure.

"You little idiot," he muttered, moving forward to force open her hand.

She let him, numb, her eyes falling to the sight of his dark hands under her pale one where blood beaded from a small cut.

"I . . . wasn't expecting . . . you," she said nervously.

"Obviously. Do you have some antiseptic?"

"In the bathroom."

He marched her into it and fumbled in the medicine cabinet for antiseptic and a bandage.

"Where's Ada?" he asked as he cleaned the small cut, examined it for shards, and applied the stinging antiseptic.

"Out getting pizza," she muttered.

He glanced up. He'd never been so close to her, and those silver eyes at point-blank range were frightening. So was the warmth of his lean, powerful body and the smell of his musky cologne.

His eyes searched hers quietly, and he didn't smile. That wasn't unusual. She'd only seen him smile at Ada or his mother. He was reserved to the point of inhibition most of the time. A hard man. Cold...

Something wild and frightening dilated her eyes as she met that long, lingering look, and her heart jumped. Her lips parted as she tore her gaze down to the small hand that was visibly trembling in his big ones.

"Nervous, Katriane?" he asked.

"Yes, I'm nervous," she bit off, deciding that a lie would only amuse him. If granite could be amused.

"How long did it take Ada to talk you into this visit?" he asked.

She drew in a heavy breath. "All of a half hour," she said gruffly. "And I still think it's a horrible mistake." She looked up at him defiantly. "I don't want to spoil Christmas for her by fighting with you."

His chin lifted as he studied her. "Then you'll just have to be nice to me, won't you?" he baited. "No snide remarks, no deliberate taunts..."

"Look who's talking about snide remarks!" she returned. "You're the one who does all the attacking!"

"You give as good as you get, don't you?" he asked.

Her lower lip jutted. "It's Christmas."

"Yes, I know." He studied her. "I like presents."

"Is anyone going to give you one?" she asked incredulously.

"Ada," he reminded her.

"Poor demented soul, she loves you," she said, eyeing him.

"Women do, from time to time," he returned.

"Ah, the advantages of wealth," she muttered.

"Do you think I have to pay for it?" he asked with a cold smile. "I suppose a woman who sells it expects everyone to..."

Her hand lifted again, but he caught it this time, holding it so that she had to either stand on her tiptoes or have her shoulder dislocated.

"Let go!" she panted. "You're hurting!"

"Then stop trying to hit me. Peace on earth, remember?" he reminded her, oddly calm.

"I'd like to leave you in pieces," she mumbled, glaring up at him.

His eyes wandered from her wild, waving red-gold hair down past her full breasts to her small waist, flaring hips and long legs. "You've gained a little weight, haven't you?" he asked. "As voluptuous as ever. I suppose that appeals to some men."

"Ooooh!" she burst out, infuriated, struggling.

He let her go all at once and pulled a cigarette from his pocket, watching her with amusement as he lit it. "What's the matter? Disappointed because you don't appeal to me?"

"God forbid!"

He shook his head. "You'll have to do better than this if you want to keep a truce with me for the next few days. I can't tolerate hysterical women."

She closed her eyes, willing him to disappear. It didn't work. When she opened them, he was still there. She put away the antiseptic and bandages and went back into the living room, walking stiffly, to clean the debris of the shattered ball from the beige carpet.

"Don't cut yourself," he cautioned, dropping lazily into an armchair with the ashtray he'd found.

"On what, the ball or you?" she asked coldly.

He only laughed, softly, menacingly; and she fumbled with pieces of the ball while he watched her in that catlike, unblinking way of his.

"I thought Ada told me you'd stopped smoking," she remarked when she was finished.

"I did. I only do it now when I'm nervous." He took another long draw, his eyes mocking. "You give me the jitters, honey, didn't you know?"

"Me and the cobalt bomb, maybe," she scoffed. She threw away the debris and ran an irritated hand through her hair. "Do you want me to show you to your room, like a good hostess?" she asked.

"You'd show me to the elevator and press the Down button," he said. "I'll wait for my sister and a warmer welcome."

It was Christmas, and he'd lost his mother, and she hated the surge of sympathy she felt. But knowing he'd toss it right back in her face kept her quiet. She went to the window and stared down at the busy street. "Ada, hurry," she wanted to scream.

"I saw your book advertised on television the other day," he remarked.

She turned around, arms folded defensively over her breasts. "Did you? Imagine, you watching television."

He didn't take her up on that. He crushed out his half-finished cigarette. "It sold out at the local bookstore."

"I'm sure you bought all the copies—to keep your good neighbors from being exposed to it," she chided.

His eyebrows arched. "In fact, I did buy one copy. To read."

She went red from head to toe. The thought of Egan Winthrop reading *Harvest of Passion* made her want to pull a blanket over her head. It was a spicy book with sensuous love scenes, and the way he was looking her over made it obvious what he thought of the book and its author.

"I like historical fiction," he remarked. "Despite having to wade through the obligatory sex to get to it."

She flushed even more and turned away, too tongue-tied to answer him.

"How do you manage to stay on your feet with all that exhaustive research you obviously do?"

She whirled, her eyes blazing. "What do you mean by that?" she burst out.

He laughed softly, predatorily. "You know damned good and well what I mean. How many men does it take?"

The door opened just in time to spare his ears. Ada walked in and her face glowed with joy as she saw her brother. She tossed the pizza onto a chair and ran to him, to be swung up in his powerful arms and warmly kissed.

"You get prettier all the time," he said, laughing, and the radiance in his face made

Kati feel like mourning. She'd never bring that look to Egan's face.

"And you get handsomer. I'm so glad you could come," Ada said genuinely.

"I'm glad someone is," he murmured, glancing at Kati's flushed, furious face.

Ada looked past him, and her own expression sobered. "Ooops," she murmured.

Kati swallowed her hostility. She wouldn't ruin Christmas for Ada—she wouldn't. She pinned a smile to her lips. "It's all right. He patched me up when I cut my hand. We're friends now. Aren't we?" she asked, grinding her teeth together as she looked at Egan.

"Of course," he agreed. "Bosom pals." He stared at her breasts.

Ada grabbed him by the hand and half dragged him from the room. "Let me show you where to put your suitcase, Egan!" she said hastily.

Kati went to take the pizza into the kitchen and make coffee. And counted to ten, five times.

Chapter Two

"How have you been?" Ada asked her brother as the three of them sat around the dining room table munching pizza and drinking coffee.

"All right," he said, staring at the thick brown mug that held his coffee. "You?"

Ada smiled. "Busy. It's helped me not to dwell on Mama."

"She's better off," Egan reminded her quietly.

"I know," Ada said, her eyes misting. She shook her head and grabbed another slice of pizza. "Anybody else for seconds? There are three slices left."

"No more for me," Kati said with a speaking glance at Egan. "I wouldn't want to get more voluptuous than I already am."

"Nonsense," blissfully ignorant Ada said. "You're just right. Come on, have another slice."

"Go ahead," Egan taunted.

"Why don't you?" she dared him.

"And be accused of making a pig of myself?" he asked innocently.

"Who would be so unkind as to call you a pig?" Kati asked sweetly.

"Excuse me," Ada interrupted, "but it's Christmas. Remember? Holly and mistletoe . . . ?"

"Mistletoe?" Egan glanced at Kati. "I'd rather drink poison."

Kati glared back. "Ditto!"

"Let's watch television!" Ada suggested frantically. She dragged Kati into the living room and quickly turned on the set. "I'll clear the table, you keep Egan company."

"You're just afraid of getting caught in the line of fire," Egan accused as his sister rushed out of the room.

But Ada only grinned.

Egan eased down into the armchair he'd vacated earlier and stared at Kati. He'd taken off his coat and vest. Both sleeves of his white silk shirt were rolled up and the neck was opened. He didn't wear an undershirt, and through the thin fabric, bronzed muscles and a thick pelt of hair were visible. That bothered Kati, so she carefully avoided looking at him while the evening news blared into the room.

"How's the writing going?" Egan asked conversationally.

"Just fine, thanks," she replied tersely.

"What are you working on now?"

She swallowed. Ada had finked on her, she just knew it. "Actually, I'm doing another historical."

"On . . . ?"

She cleared her throat. "Wyoming," she mumbled.

"Pardon?" he said.

Her lips made a thin line. "Wyoming," she said louder.

"A historical novel about Wyoming. Well, well. Have you done a lot of research?"

She glanced at him warily. "What do you mean?"

"Historical research," he clarified, watching her. "You'll have to mention cattle-ranching, I imagine?"

"Yes," she said grudgingly.

"Know a lot about it, city lady?" he mocked.

She glared at him. "I have been on a ranch before."

"Sure. Mine." He stared down his nose at her. "I don't imagine they have many big cattle ranches in Charleston?"

"We have good people," she returned. "With excellent breeding."

His eyebrows arched. "Yes, I know. My grandmother came from Charleston."

She glared at him. "Did she, really?" she asked coldly.

He smiled softly. "She used to say it was where the Cooper and Ashley Rivers meet to form the Atlantic Ocean."

She'd heard that, too, in her childhood in the South Carolina coastal city, and she had to bite her lip to keep from smiling with him.

"She was a redhead too," he continued, waiting for a reaction.

"My hair isn't red," she said, predictably.

"Honey and fox fur," he argued, studying it.

She flushed. That sounded oddly poetic, and she didn't like the tingle that ran through her.

She glanced at her watch. "Excuse me. I'd better put on a dress."

Egan glared. "Going somewhere?"

"Yes." She left him sitting there and went to find Ada. "Jack's coming for me at seven," she reminded her friend. "I've got to get dressed."

"I'll go keep Egan company. Lucky you, to have a boyfriend in town." She sighed. "Mine's out at sea again."

"Marshal will be back before you know it," she murmured. "Sorry to run out on you."

"You'll have fun." Ada grinned. "And so will I. I like Egan. He's great company, even if he is my brother."

Well, there was no accounting for taste. She couldn't imagine Egan being great company; but then, she wasn't related to him.

She put on a black cocktail dress and wore red accessories with it. Her eyes gave her a critical appraisal. She'd twirled her hair into a French twist and added a rhinestone clip to it, and she liked that elegant touch. She grinned. Jack would love it.

Jack Asher was a reporter for *The New York Times,* a political specialist who was intelligent and fun to be with. She'd known him for several months and enjoyed the occasional date. But things were still platonic between them because she didn't want any serious involvement. She was too independent.

The doorbell rang while she was putting a gloss of lipstick on her mouth, and she knew

Ada would get it. Then she remembered that Egan was here, and rushed to finish her makeup and get back into the living room.

Jack was standing in the hall, talking to Ada while Egan glared at him.

He cleared his throat when Kati joined him, looking painfully relieved to see her.

"Hi, lady," he said with a forced smile. He was blond and blue-eyed and not nearly as tall or muscular as Egan. Sadly enough, in comparison he looked rather pale and dull.

But Kati grinned at him and Ada as if nothing were wrong. "Had to find my purse, but I'm ready when you are. Night, Ada. Egan," she added, glancing his way.

Egan didn't answer her. He was still glaring at Jack with those dangerous narrowed eyes glittering like new silver while he smoked a cigarette. Ada made a frantic gesture, but he ignored her too.

"Night, Ada," Jack said uncomfortably and led Kati out the door.

"Whew!" Jack exclaimed when they reached the elevator. "I felt like an insect on a mounting board for a second there! Is he always like that? So... uncommunicative?"

"Egan?" Kati's eyes flared up. "He's usually much too communicative, if you want to know. We're stuck with him for Christmas. Ada invited him because their mother died earlier this year. She felt sorry for him, being all alone."

"I should think so," Jack said gently. "Well, maybe he talks to her." He frowned. "You don't like him, do you?"

"Not one bit. Not one ounce. Not a fraction." She glared at the elevator.

Jack laughed. "Poor guy!"

"Not Egan. Feel sorry for me. I'm stuck in the same apartment with him for the next week," she moaned.

"You could always move in with me," he offered.

She laughed, knowing the offer was a joke, just as it always had been. They didn't have that kind of relationship. "Sure I could. I can just see your mother's face."

"Mother likes you." He chuckled. "She'd probably be thrilled."

"Only because she could pump me for my latest plots." She grinned. "You know she's one of my biggest fans. Sweet lady."

"She's sweet, all right. Well, where do you want to go? The Rainbow Grill?"

"Let's save it for a special time. How about the Crawdaddy Room at the Roosevelt?"

He chuckled. "You just like to go there because of their pudding," he accused.

"Well, it is terribly good," she reminded him.

"I know, I know. Actually, I like it myself."

She followed him into the elevator and put the confrontation with Egan right out of her mind.

A prime rib, a salad, several hard rolls and a dish of delicious whiskey pudding later, Kati sat drinking her coffee and looking around at the elegant surroundings. She saw a nice little old German waiter she knew from other visits there and smiled at him.

"Friend of yours?" Jack asked her.

"Everybody's my friend." She laughed. "I used to think New York was a cold place until I moved here. New Yorkers just take a little getting to know. And then they're family. I love New York," she sang softly, and laughed again.

"So do I. Of course, I was born here," he added. He looked out the window at the traffic. "I've got tickets for a modern ballet, if you'd like to use them."

"Could we?"

"Sure. Come on."

He led her down a side street where a group of people were just entering what looked like an old warehouse. But inside, it was a theater, complete with live orchestra and lighted stage and some of the most beautiful modern ballet she'd ever watched. The people onstage looked like living art: the women delicate and pink in their tulle and satin, the men vigorous and athletic and vibrant. Kati had been going to the ballet for years, but this was something special.

Afterward, they went to a lounge and drank piña coladas and danced to the hazy music of a combo until the wee hours.

"That was fun," she told Jack when he brought her home. "We'll have to do it again."

"Indeed we will. I'm sorry I didn't think of the ballet weeks ago. I get free tickets."

"Let's do it again even if we have to pay for them," she said, laughing.

"Suits me. I'll call you in a few days. Looks like I may have to fly down to Washington on that latest scandal."

"Call me when you get back, okay?"

"Okay. Night, doll." He winked and was gone. He never tried to kiss her or make advances. With them, it was friendship instead of involvement, and she enjoyed his company very much. Jack had been married and his wife had died. He wanted involvement even less than she did and was glad to be going out with someone who wouldn't try to tie him up in wedding paper.

Dreamily, she unlocked the apartment door and stepped inside. She closed the door and leaned back against it, humming a few bars of the classical piece that had accompanied one of the pieces at the ballet.

"Do you usually stay out this late?" Egan asked from the living room. He was standing by the window with a glass of amber liquid that looked like whiskey in his hand.

She stared at him. "I'm twenty-five," she reminded him. "I stay out as late as I like."

He moved toward her slowly, gracefully, his eyes holding hers. "Do you sleep with him?" he asked.

She caught her breath. "Egan, what I do with anyone is my business."

He threw back the rest of his drink and set the glass on a small table in the hall, moving toward her until she felt like backing away.

"How is he?" he asked lazily. Then he caught her by the shoulders and held her in front of him, looking down quietly, holding her eyes.

Her lips parted as she met that intimidating stare. "Egan..."

His nostrils flared. The lean fingers that were holding her tightened. "Is he white all over?'' he continued in a faintly mocking tone. "City boy."

"Well, there aren't many cattle to herd up here," she said tautly.

"No, but there are too damn many people. You can't walk two steps without running into someone," he complained. "I couldn't survive here. Answer me. Do you sleep with him?"

"That's non—" she began.

"Tell me anyway. Does he do all those things to you that you write about in your books?" he asked, studying her. "Does he 'strip you slowly,' so that you can 'feel every brush of his fingers...'"

"Egan!" She reached up to press her fingers against his lips, stopping the words as she flushed deeply.

He hadn't expected the touch of her fingers. He caught them and held them as if he wasn't sure what to do with them. His eyes held hers.

"Is that the kind of man you like, Katriane Desiree?" he asked, using the full name that she didn't know he'd ever heard.

She watched him helplessly. "I like...
writers," she managed.

"Do you?" He brought her hand to his
mouth and kissed its warm palm softly,
slowly. His teeth nipped at her slender fore-
finger.

"Egan," she breathed nervously.

He took the tip of her finger into his
mouth and she felt his tongue touching it.
"Afraid?" he murmured. "Don't they say
that a woman is instinctively afraid of a man
she thinks can conquer her?"

She wrenched away from him like an animal at bay. "You'd be lucky!" she whispered. Was that her voice, shaking like that?

He stared at her, sliding his hands into his
pockets, and the action stretched the fabric
of his trousers tight over the powerful muscles of his legs. "So would you," he returned. "But one of these days I might give
you a thrill, honey. God knows, my taste
never ran to virgins. And an experienced
woman is...exciting."

She felt the blood rush into her face, and
she whirled on her heel. If she stayed there

one second longer, she'd hit him! Boy, wouldn't the joke be on him if he ever tried to take her to bed! Egan, in bed. . . .

She went straight into the bathroom, oblivious that she might wake Ada, and ran herself a calming cool shower.

Chapter Three

Kati didn't sleep. Every time she closed her eyes, she could feel the hard grip of Egan's fingers on her shoulders, the touch of his mouth against her hand. She hated him, she thought miserably; that was why she couldn't sleep.

She dragged into the kitchen just after daylight, with her long gold and beige striped caftan flowing lovingly over the soft curves of her body. Her tousled hair fell in glorious disarray around her shoulders, and her dark eyes were even darker with drowsiness.

With a long yawn, she filled the coffee pot and started it, then she reached for the skillet and bacon and turned on the stove. She was leaning back against the refrigerator with a carton of eggs in one hand and butter in the other when the kitchen door opened and Egan came in, dressed in nothing but a pair of tan slacks.

He stopped at the sight of her and stared. She did some staring of her own. He was just as she'd imagined him without that shirt—sexy as all get-out. Bronzed muscles rippled as he closed the kitchen door; a mat of hair on his chest curled down obviously below his belt buckle. His arms looked much more powerful without a concealing shirt, as did his shoulders. She could hardly drag her eyes away.

"I thought I'd fix myself a cup of coffee," he said quietly.

"I just put some on," she said.

He cocked an eyebrow. "Does that mean I have to wait until you drink your potful before I can make mine?" he asked.

She glared at him. So much for truces. "There's a nice little coffee shop down on the corner," she suggested with a venomous smile.

"I'll tell Ada you're being unkind to me," he threatened. "Remember Ada? My sister? The one whose Christmas you said you didn't want to spoil?"

She drew in a calming breath. "Do excuse me, Mr. Winthrop," she said formally. "Wouldn't you like to sit down; I'll pour you a cup of coffee."

"Not until you tell me where you plan to pour it," he returned.

"Don't tempt me." She reached up into the cabinet for a second cup and saucer while he pulled out a chair and straddled it.

When she turned back with the filled cups, she found him watching her. It unnerved her when he did that, and she spilled coffee into one of the saucers before she could set them on the table.

"Couldn't you sleep?" he asked pleasantly.

"No," she said. "I'm not used to sleeping late. I'm at my best early in the morning."

A slow, wicked smile touched his hard mouth. "Most of us are," he commented.

It didn't necessarily mean what she thought it did, but she couldn't help the blush. And that increased her embarrassment, because he laughed.

"Will you stop!" she burst out, glaring at him. "Oh, why don't you take your coffee and go back to bed?"

"I'm hungry. Don't I smell bacon?"

"Bacon!" She jumped up and turned it just in time. It was a nice golden brown.

"Going to scramble some eggs, too?" he asked.

"No, I thought I'd let you drink yours raw," she said.

He only laughed, sipping his coffee. "I like raw oysters, but I draw the line at raw eggs. Want me to make the toast?"

"You can cook?"

"Don't get insulting." He stood up and found the bread and butter. "Get me a pan and some cinnamon and sugar."

She stared at him.

"Cinnamon," he said patiently. "It's a spice—"

"I know what it is," she grumbled, finding it. "Here. And I've lined the pan with aluminum foil. It's all yours."

"Ungrateful woman," he muttered as he mixed the cinnamon and sugar in the shaker she'd handed him. He buttered the bread and spread the mixture on top.

"Don't get conceited just because you can make cinnamon toast," she mumbled. "After all, it isn't exactly duckling *a l'orange.*"

"I'd like to see you cook that," he remarked.

She cleared her throat. "Well, I could if I had a recipe."

"So could I." He turned on the oven and slid the toast in under the broiler. "Get me a pot holder."

"Who was your personal slave yesterday?" she asked, tossing him a quilted pot holder.

"I liked the old days," he murmured, glancing at her. "When men hunted and women cooked and had kids."

"Drudgery," she scoffed. "Women were little more than free labor...."

"Cosseted and protected and worried over and loved to death," he continued, staring down at her. "Now they're overbearing, pushy, impossible to get along with and wilder than bucks."

"Look who's talking about being wild!" she burst out.

He stared down his nose at her. "I'm a man."

She drew in a breath and let it out, and her eyes involuntarily ran over him.

"No argument?" he asked.

She turned away. "Your toast's burning."

He took it out—nicely browned and smelling sweet and delicate—and put it on a plate while she scrambled eggs.

"I like mine fried, honey," he commented.

"Okay. There's a frying pan; grease is in the cabinet. If you're too good to eat my scrambled eggs, you can mutilate your own any way you like."

He chuckled softly, an odd sound that she'd never heard, and she turned to look up at him.

"Firecracker," he murmured, his eyes narrow and searching. "Are you like that in bed?"

She jerked her eyes away and concentrated on the eggs. "Wouldn't you like to get dressed before we eat?"

It was a mistake. A horrible mistake. Because then he knew what she hadn't admitted since he walked into the room. That, stripped to the waist, he bothered her.

The arrogant beast knew it, all right. He moved lazily until he was standing just behind her... so close that she felt him and smelled him and wanted nothing more out of life than to turn around and slide her hands all over that broad chest.

His hands caught her waist, making her jump, and eased her back against him so that she could feel the warm, hard muscles of his chest and stomach against her back. The caftan was paper-thin, and it was like standing naked in his arms.

She felt his fingers move to her hips, caressingly, and her hand trembled as it stirred the eggs to keep them from burning.

"Egan, don't," she whispered shakily.

His breath was warm and rough in her hair, because the top of her head only came to his chin. The fingers holding her hips contracted, and she felt the tips of them on her flat stomach like a brand.

"Put down that damned spoon and turn around," he said in a tone she didn't recognize.

She was shaking like a leaf, and God only knew what would have happened. But noisy footsteps sounded outside the kitchen door, and an equally noisy yawn followed it. Egan let go of her and moved away just as Ada walked in.

"There you are!" she said brightly, watching her best friend stir eggs. "I'm starved!"

"It'll be on the table in two shakes," Kati promised, hoping her voice didn't sound as shaky as it felt. Damn Egan!

"I'd better get dressed," Egan commented, winking at Ada as he went past her. "I think I bother somebody like this."

Kati made an unforgivable comment under her breath as he left the room.

"At it again, I see," Ada sighed wearily.

"He started it," Kati said through her teeth. "I didn't ask him to walk in here naked."

"What?" Ada blinked.

Kati looked at her friend with a pained expression. "Oh God, isn't he beautiful?" she whispered with genuine feeling.

Ada chuckled gleefully. "Well, I always thought so, even if he is my brother. But isn't that something of a strange admission for you to make?"

"It slipped out. Just forget it." She dished up the eggs. "I think I'd better put something on too."

"Don't be long," Ada cautioned. "The eggs will congeal."

"I'll hurry."

She ran for her bedroom and closed the door just as Egan opened his. A minute's grace! She got into her jeans, blue T-shirt and shoes, and barely stopped to run a brush through her hair. She hoped it would be a short week. She hadn't expected Egan to have this kind of effect on her. In all the years she'd known him, he'd never even tried to make a pass at her. Now, in less than two days, he'd made more impact on her guarded emotions than any other man had in all her twenty-five years. She was going to have to get a hold on herself. She didn't know what kind of game Egan had in mind, but she wasn't playing.

He was wearing a brown velour pullover when she came back, one that emphasized his dark hair and complexion and the hard muscles she'd already seen.

"We left a little for you," Egan commented as she sat down. He pushed aside his empty plate and poured himself another cup of coffee from the hotplate on the table.

"How kind of you," she said pleasantly. She held up her cup and Egan filled it, studying her far too closely.

"What does your boyfriend do for a living?" he asked unexpectedly.

"Jack isn't my boyfriend," she said. "He's a man I date. And he's a political reporter for *The New York Times*."

He leaned back in his chair while Ada bit her lower lip and looked apprehensive.

"Is he really?" Egan asked. "He doesn't look like he gets much exercise. A little overweight, wouldn't you say?"

She glared at him. "He works very hard."

He only laughed, and sipped his coffee. "If I took him home with me, I could break him in one day."

"You could break the devil in one day," Kati said, exasperated. "What business is it of yours who I date?"

"Now, that's a good question," he replied. His eyes narrowed, and there was a smile she didn't understand on his chiseled lips. "Maybe I feel sorry for the poor man. He does know what you do for a living, doesn't he? Must be hell on him, having everything he does to you turn up in a book...."

"Egan." Ada groaned, hiding her face in her hands.

"You overbearing, unspeakable, mean tempered..." Kati began in a low tone. She threw her napkin down onto the table and stood up.

"You sure got up on the wrong side of the bed," Egan commented. "Here I am a guest in your apartment—"

"I'd sooner invite a cobra to breakfast!" she burst out.

"You should have," he murmured, glancing at the plate he'd just emptied. "He might have enjoyed burned eggs and half-raw bacon."

She tried to speak, couldn't, and just stormed out of the room.

She left the apartment before Ada could get out of the kitchen, and wandered around the streets shivering in her thin jacket for an hour before she gave up and went back. It was too cold for pride, anyway. All she'd accomplished was to let Egan see how unreasonably she reacted to his prodding. She'd just have to grit her teeth, for Ada's sake.

Egan was nowhere in sight when she got back, and Ada looked apologetic and worn.

"I don't understand him, I just don't," Ada groaned. "Oh Kati, I'm sorry. If I'd realized how bad things were between you, I'd never have invited him."

Kati was generous enough not to remind her friend that she'd tried to warn her. She sat down on the sofa with a hard sigh.

"I'll manage. Where is he?" she added darkly.

"Gone to spend the day with some girl friend of his," Ada said absently. "He said he might not be back until late."

Why that simple statement should make her feel murderous, Kati didn't know. But something gnawed inside her at the thought of Egan with another woman.

"I wonder how much he had to bribe her?" she asked nastily.

"Shame on you," Ada said.

But Kati didn't apologize. And she didn't dwell on her confused emotions, either. She wanted no complications in her life, especially with someone like Egan Winthrop.

She and Ada went shopping later in the day and ate out at a little Italian restaurant just down the street from their apartment. They watched television and eventually went to bed. And Egan didn't come back. Not that night. Not until the next morning.

Kati was sitting on the living room floor with pages littering the area around her. They were galleys of her latest book, which had come that morning by special messenger, and she was going over them. Ada was at auditions for a new play, hoping to be home by lunch if she didn't get held up at the theater during tryouts. That was a laugh. Most of the time, it took hours. Despite the appointments the hopefuls were given, something always went wrong. Ada had never gotten back when she thought she would, and Kati was dreading Egan's arrival. She felt wild when she thought of his not coming in at all, and angry because she didn't understand why. She didn't even *like* the man, for God's sake!

There was a loud knock at the door an hour later, and when she opened it, Egan was standing there looking faintly amused and as immaculate as when he'd left. Still in the same clothes, of course....

She glared at him. "Lose your key?" she asked.

"I thought I'd better not use it, in case you were ... entertaining," he said.

She let him in, slammed the door and went back to her comfortable sprawl on the floor.

"Coffee's hot if you want some," she said icily. "I'm busy reading."

"Don't let me interrupt you. I thought I'd have a quick shower and change clothes. I've got a lunch date."

Why oh why did she feel like smashing plates? She frowned and concentrated on what she was doing. Minutes later, he was back, dressed in a navy blue pinstripe suit with a white silk shirt and a blue and burgundy tie. He looked regal. Sexy. Unbelievably handsome for such an ugly man. If he was dressing like that in the middle of the day, he must be on his way to the Waldorf, she thought. And God only knew with whom.

"Ada didn't worry, did she?" he asked, checking his watch.

"Oh, no. She's used to people staying out all night," she lied deliberately, lifting her eyes. It shocked her, the flash of reaction in his face before it was quickly erased.

His eyes ran over her: the gray slacks and burgundy silk blouse she was wearing, her feet hose-clad and without shoes. Her hair was loose, and flowed in waves of reddish gold silk down her shoulders; her face was rosy and full of life.

His scrutiny made her nervous, and she dropped her eyes back to the page she was reading.

He moved closer and suddenly bent to pick up a page. His eyebrows rose as he read, and a slow smile touched his mouth.

"You do put your heart into it, don't you?" he murmured.

She reached up and took the page out of his hands, glancing at it. She blushed and tucked it under what she was reading. Why did he have to pick up *that* page? she groaned inwardly.

"Is that what you like with a man?" he continued maddeningly, his hands in his pockets, his eyes intent. "I've never done it in a bathtub, but I suppose—"

"Will you please go away?" she groaned, letting her hair fall over her eyes. "I don't care where you've done it, or with whom, just please go eat your lunch and leave me to my sordid occupation."

"I suppose I'd better. Stockbrokers sure as hell don't have time to waste."

She looked up as he turned to leave. "Stockbroker?" she murmured incredulously.

He glanced down at her from his formidable height with an expression she couldn't decipher. "I'm a businessman," he reminded her. "I do have the odd investment to look after."

"Yes, I know," she said quickly. "I just thought—"

"That because I was out all night, it was with a woman—and that I was meeting her for a leisurely lunch?" he suggested in a menacing tone.

She turned back to her work, trying to ignore him. It wasn't easy when he loomed over her that way.

"The reasons I stayed away might shock you, city girl," he said after a minute.

"I don't doubt it for a minute," she muttered.

"And that wasn't what I meant. It might have something to do with you."

The careless remark brought her eyes up, and he held them relentlessly for so long that she felt currents singing through her body.

"I didn't expect you to start trembling the minute I put my hands on you," he said in a harsh undertone. "Not after all these years. We've been enemies."

"We still are," she said in what she hoped was a convincing tone, while humiliation stuck like bile in her throat.

"Dead right," he said coldly. "And it's going to stay that way. I don't want complications during this holiday."

"Ditto," she said curtly. "And don't go around flattering your ego too much, Egan," she added. "I was half asleep at the time!"

His darkened eyes searched hers in the stillness that followed, and she was aware of him in a way she'd never been aware of a man before. Of his height and strength, of the devastating effect he had on her senses.

"Saving your pride, Kati?" he asked quietly.

She studied her long fingernails. "I like my life as it is," she said. "I'm on the go too much for relationships of any kind. And what you'd have in mind ... !" she began.

"Now who's flattering their ego?" he asked shortly, glaring down at her. "My

God, I don't mind experience in my women, but I draw the line at promiscuity!''

She scrambled to her feet and was ready to swing when the dark look on his face worked some kind of witchcraft and left her standing helplessly with her fists clenched.

''You slapped me once and got away with it,'' he said quietly. ''If you do it again now, we'll wind up in bed together.''

She felt her body tremble at the words. ''No,'' she bit off.

''Yes.'' His chest rose and fell heavily, and his eyes cut into hers. ''Don't you realize that the way we react to each other is like flint and steel? All it would take is a kiss. Just that. And we'd burn each other alive. I've known that from the very beginning.''

She hadn't, and the thought of Egan as a lover made her face burn. She had to smother a gasp as she turned away with her arms folded protectively around her slender body.

''Don't worry. You're safe, city girl,'' he said in a mocking tone. ''I'm not that desperate. Just don't push me too far.''

She couldn't even face what he was insinuating. Egan was the enemy. He was going to stay that way too, if she had to bite her tongue in two. She stared blankly out the window.

"And it's Ada that's auditioning for acting jobs," he commented sarcastically. "Playing innocent?"

She didn't have to play, but he'd never believe it. He'd just shocked her to her nylon-clad feet, and she was lost for words. It was a little frightening to be threatened with a man's bed, just for provoking him. She hadn't been aware that she *was* provoking him until now. Which automatically led to her asking why she did it, and that was frightening as well.

"Kati," he called softly.

She stiffened. "Will your stockbroker wait?" she asked quietly.

He frowned at her stiff back. "What the hell's the matter with you?"

"You threaten me with sex and then ask me what's wrong?" she burst out, staring at him nervously over one shoulder.

He blinked, as if she'd shocked him. "It wasn't a threat."

She flushed and walked away.

"Will you stop doing your Lady Innocent act and look at me?" he growled.

She walked into her bedroom and slammed the door. On an afterthought, she locked it, too. There was a string of unprintable curses from the vicinity of the living room before the front door slammed violently and the room became quiet.

It wasn't going to be possible to stay in the same apartment with Egan after this, she thought miserably. She'd just have to check into a hotel until he left. Having to put up with his incessant verbal aggression was bad enough; but when he started threatening to make it physical, that was the end. The very end.

The conceited beast—to accuse her of being so vulnerable that she'd jump into his bed at the first opportunity. She groaned as she recalled the touch of his hands on her hips, the wild tremors that had run through her untried body. She gritted her teeth. She'd have to get away from him. Because what if he did that again? The real problem was telling Ada she was leaving without spoiling the poor girl's Christmas.

Chapter Four

Kati had half her clothes in her suitcase by the time Ada came home from her tryout. She still hadn't decided what she was going to do, beyond checking into a hotel down the street. She knew for certain that she couldn't take one more night of Egan.

"What are you doing?" Ada asked hesitantly, pausing in the doorway of Kati's room.

"Cleaning out my drawers," came the terse reply.

Ada cleared her throat. "Where are you taking what was in them?"

"To a hotel."

Ada leaned back against the doorjamb wearily. "Egan came home."

"How did you ever guess?" Kati asked pleasantly. She closed the lid of the suitcase.

"You're adults," Ada argued. "Surely you should be able to get along just during Christmas holidays? Peace on earth?"

"There is no peace where your brother is," Kati said vehemently. She tossed back a strand of hair and glared across the room. "I find it no less than miraculous that he can get people to work for him at all!"

The other woman sighed. "Amazingly enough, most of the hands have been with him for years. He has hardly any turnover." She glanced at Kati. "And he gets along wonderfully with women, as a rule. Polite, courteous, attentive—"

"We are talking about the same man?" Kati had to ask. "The big ugly one who's been staying here for two days and one night?"

Ada shook her head, laughing. "Oh, Kati. Kati." She moved out into the hall. "You win. I'll pack, too. We'll let Egan have the apartment and we'll both go to a hotel."

"Now hold on," Kati protested. "It's Christmas, and he's your brother, and the whole point of asking him here—"

"Was not to ruin your Christmas, believe it or not," Ada said gently. "You're like a sister to me. How can I let you leave alone?"

Kati bit her lower lip and stared helplessly at the suitcase. She didn't know what to do anymore.

"Maybe if you pretend he's not here?" Ada suggested softly.

Kati looked up. "He won't let me. He keeps making horrible remarks; he says..." Her face flushed, and she couldn't meet the curious look in her friend's eyes. "He has this strange idea about where I get material for my books."

"Suppose I talk to him?"

"That would make it worse." She moved the suitcase aside and sat down heavily. "I'll stay. I can't come between the two of you, not at Christmas."

"You're a doll." Ada grinned.

"I wish I were. Maybe then he'd let me alone," came the muttered reply.

"Just treat him like someone you've never met before," Ada suggested.

"That's an idea."

"Anything's worth trying once."

"Yes. Where do you keep the arsenic?"

"Shame on you! It's Christmas!"

"All right, I'm easy," Kati agreed. "Where's the holly stake?"

Ada threw up her hands and left the room.

It was late that evening when Egan came in, looking disheveled and out of sorts. He glared at Kati as if every ill in the world could be laid at her feet.

"We, uh, saved you some supper, Egan," Ada said.

"I'm not hungry," he returned gruffly, but his eyes still didn't leave Kati.

"I'll bring you some coffee," Kati said pleasantly and with a polite smile.

Egan stared after her blankly. "Concussion?" he asked Ada.

Ada laughed, going to help her friend in the kitchen.

"It's working," she whispered as they filled a tray. "He thinks you're sick."

"When hasn't he?" Kati muttered. She sliced some pound cake, added some dessert plates, forks and napkins to their coffee service, and carried the loaded tray into the living room.

Egan was sprawled in the big armchair that he'd appropriated since his arrival. He glared up from its depths as Kati put the tray down on the coffee table.

"I said I wasn't hungry," he repeated.

"Oh, the cake isn't for you," Kati said sweetly. "It's for Ada and me."

That seemed to make him worse. He sat up and took the cup of black coffee Kati poured him, sipping it. He seemed to brighten all at once. "Too weak," he said, staring at her.

She ignored the challenge. "Is it?" She tasted hers. "Yes," she lied, "it certainly is. I'll make some more."

"Don't bother," he returned curtly, leaning back with the cup and saucer held on the palm of one large, lean hand. "It'll do."

She nibbled at her cake and idly watched television. The program they had chosen was a romantic comedy about detectives.

"Isn't he dashing?" Ada sighed as the leading man came into view.

"Oh, rather," Kati said theatrically. "So handsome." She glanced at Egan with a lifted eyebrow.

Egan glanced back at her with hard eyes. But he didn't say a word.

"Did you settle that business with our stockbroker?" Ada asked when the commercial came on.

"Yes," Egan replied curtly. He finished his coffee and stood up. "I think I'll get some sleep. It's been a trying day. Good night." He walked out without a word to Kati.

"It's barely nine," Ada murmured, scowling after him. "Egan never goes to bed this early."

"Maybe it's his conscience bothering him," Kati suggested. "About the abominable way he's been treating me?"

"Dream on, my best friend," came the sighing reply.

The phone rang and Ada dragged herself over to answer it, brightening when she heard the caller. "It's Marshal!" she whispered to Kati.

Kati grinned. Ada's boyfriend had been away for several weeks, and the joy of homecoming was in her eyes. She moved the phone into the hall while Kati finished watching television.

"He wants us to double up tomorrow night at the Rainbow Grill. Want to ask Jack?" Ada asked.

"I'd love to, but Jack's still out of town. How about Friday night?"

"Fine! I'll make sure it's okay with Marshal."

"You'll make sure what's okay?" Egan asked, stopping in the doorway with his tie in his hand and his shirt unbuttoned over his broad chest.

"A date, Friday night," Ada volunteered. "Want to come along? I've got a super girl friend—"

"I can get my own women," he said with a tilt of his mouth. "Friday? I'll ask Jennie. What time?"

Kati's heart sank, and it showed in her eyes. Egan happened to look her way; he smiled with pure malice.

"What's the matter, honey, will I cramp your style if I come along?" he asked her.

Kati remembered almost too late the role she'd chosen to play. Polite hostess. No personalities. No hostilities. Christmas. Good cheer.

She gritted her teeth. "You're welcome, of course," she said with a frozen smile.

Egan's heavy eyebrows lifted. "My God, get a doctor," he told Ada.

Kati smiled even brighter. "Now, I think I'll say good night, too. I have this headache..."

"But it's only nine," Ada wailed. "Don't both of you go to bed and leave me alone."

"Don't you want peace and quiet?" Egan asked his sister.

Ada glanced from one to the other of them and sighed. "Well, I think I'll come, too. I need my beauty sleep, I guess."

"Some of us might benefit from it," Kati muttered, glaring up at Egan.

He chuckled softly. "Think I'm ugly?"

She flushed. Her eyes involuntarily ran over the craggy contours, the broken nose, the hard, cruel mouth. For some odd reason, she couldn't quite look away. His eyes caught and held hers, and they stood staring at each other in a silence that blazed with new tensions.

"Excuse me," Ada murmured, trying to hide a grin as she edged past Kati's frozen form and into her own bedroom. "Good night!"

Egan's chest was rising and falling roughly as he stared down at Kati. "Do you?" he asked in an odd tone.

She swallowed. Her throat felt as if it were full of cactus. Her lips parted, and Egan watched them hungrily. She realized all at once that he hadn't just been making threats earlier in the day. He wanted her!

"I...I'm tired," she managed, starting to move.

One long, hard arm came out, barring her path. "I wasn't threatening you this afternoon," he said tautly. "I was telling you how it would be. You can't be blind enough not to see how we are with each other, Kati," he added half under his breath.

She moved gingerly away from that long arm. "I... have a boyfriend... whom I like very much," she said shakily.

He eased forward, just enough to let her feel the warm strength of his body, the heat of his breath against her reddish gold hair. "Liking isn't enough."

Her eyes came up to meet his. "Isn't it?"

His fingertips touched her throat like a breath, feeling its silky texture, stroking it sensuously. "You smell of roses," he said in a husky whisper.

Her fingers caught his, trembling coldly against their warm strength as she tried to lift them away from her throat.

He caught her hand and moved it to his chest—easing it under the fabric and against thick hair and warm muscle—and her breath jerked in her throat. He felt as solid as a wall, and the wiry pelt of hair tickled her fingers as he flattened them against him. His expensive cologne filled her nostrils, drowning her in its masculine scent.

"Forgotten what to do, Kati?" he murmured roughly. "Shall I refresh your memory?"

She lifted her eyes dazedly to his, and they were wide and curious as they met his glittering gaze.

His head bent so that his hard face filled the world. "'She tore his shirt out of the way,'" he quoted huskily, "'and ran her fingers, trembling, over his hard, male...'!"

"No!" Recognizing the passage, she flushed hotly. Immediately, she dragged her hand away and shrank from him as if he'd burned her.

He laughed, but there was an odd sound to it, and his eyes blazed as she reached behind her for the doorknob to her room.

"Doesn't your reporter friend like having you do that to him?" he asked huskily. "Or does he prefer what comes later?"

She whirled on a sob, pushing open the door. She started to slam it, but he caught it with a powerful hand and she couldn't budge it.

"I hate you," she breathed shakily, frantic that Ada might hear them.

"So you keep telling me," he replied. "You're the one with no scruples, honey, so stop flying at me when I throw them back at you."

"I'm not what you think I am," she cried.

"No kidding?" he murmured insolently, letting his eyes punctuate the insult.

"You go to hell, you ugly cowboy!" she said furiously.

He studied her flushed face and black eyes amusedly. "Ada used to talk about her sweet-tempered, easygoing friend. Before I ever met you, I imagined a retiring little violet. You were a shock, honey."

"What do you think you were?" she returned.

He laughed softly. "No woman's ever pulled the wool over my eyes. It didn't take reading your books to tell me what kind of woman you were. All I had to do was watch you in action."

"The car broke down," she reminded him. "Richard and I had to walk for miles...!"

"Aren't you tired of lying about it? I told you," he added, letting his eyes narrow sensuously, "experienced women turn me on."

"Then why don't you go out and find the friend you spent the night with?" she retorted hotly.

His eyebrows went up and he grinned. "Did that bother you?"

She brought her heel down hard on his instep, without warning; and while he was off balance, she slammed the door and locked it.

"Kati!" he growled furiously.

"Go ahead, break it down!" she dared him. "I'll be screaming out the window until the police come!"

There was a muffled curse; a door opening; Ada's voice, almost hysterical; and Egan's, angry but conciliatory. Minutes later, two doors slammed almost simultaneously. With an angry sigh, Kati started stripping off her clothes and heading toward the shower. She was furious enough not to mind that the water was ice-cold.

Chapter Five

Egan was gone, blessedly, when Kati woke up late the next morning. Jack called to say he was back in town and asked Kati out for dinner. Grateful for the respite, she was waiting for him on pins and needles at six that afternoon.

Ada had been sympathetic about her brother's strange behavior, adding that he had a sore foot and it served him right. It was the first time Kati ever heard Ada say anything against Egan.

"Do you think I'm scandalous?" Kati asked unexpectedly when she and Jack were relaxing over coffee after a satisfying steak.

He stared at her. "You?"

"Because I write what I write," she added. "It's important."

"No, I don't think you're scandalous," he said honestly and smiled. "I think you're extremely talented, and your books are a joy to read."

"You don't think I lead a wild life?"

He only laughed. "No, I don't. What's wrong? Are you getting unpleasant letters again?"

"Oh, no. It's..." She sighed and propped her chin on her hand. "It's Egan."

"Please, don't spoil a perfect evening," he said with a restless movement. "He has a glare that could stop a clock."

"Tell me about it," she muttered. "He's giving me fits about what I write."

"Doesn't he realize the difference between fiction and fact?"

"Not if he doesn't want to," she said with a short laugh. "Egan makes up his rules as he goes along. He's a law unto himself out West.''

''I got that idea, all right.'' He studied her sad face and reached out impulsively to pat her hand. ''He'll leave after Christmas,'' he said bracingly.

''Roll on, New Year,'' she murmured, and sighed as she sipped her coffee.

They went dancing after dinner, and for a while Kati forgot all her troubles. She drew interested glances in the black dress she was wearing. It had a peasant bodice with a full, swirling skirt, and left her creamy shoulders bare. With her hair in a high coiffure, and a minimum of makeup, she wore the designer gown with a flair.

She felt on top of the world, until she went into the apartment and found Egan waiting in the hall.

''Where's lover boy?'' he asked, glaring past her at the closed door. ''Doesn't he come in for a nightcap?''

He was wearing a dress shirt rolled up to the elbows and half unbuttoned in front, with his black slacks. Obviously, he hadn't spent the evening at home, either, and his proprietary air irritated Kati even more. She was still fuming from last night.

"He doesn't wear a nightcap," she said with sweet venom, "and I don't lend mine."

His chin lifted at an arrogant angle and he looked at her long and hard, his dark eyes narrowing on her bare shoulders.

Self-conscious with him, she hunched her shoulders so that the elastic top came back into place, demurely covering everything south of her collarbone.

"Shy of me?" he asked quietly, moving forward.

She felt like running. Where was Ada, for heaven's sake? She couldn't get past him to her room to save her life, and she knew it.

"Where's Ada?" she asked quickly.

"In her room, talking to Marshal," he said. "Why? You're a big girl, now; you don't need protecting, do you?"

Oh yes, she did, but obviously she couldn't count on her best friend tonight.

She felt the impact of his rough, warm hands—with a sense of fatalism. Her body jerked under the sensation as he deliberately began to slide the fabric away from her shoulders and down.

"Isn't this how you had it?" he breathed, bending. His chest rose and fell roughly, and she drowned in the warmth of his body.

"Egan . . ." she began.

"Don't talk. Stand still." His mouth smoothed over her shoulder, leaving a fiery wake. His fingers held her upper arms, digging in as his teeth nipped slowly, tenderly at the silken flesh.

"Don't," she moaned, eyes closed, throat arching as if it invited him—begged him—to do what he pleased.

"You want it," he whispered huskily. "So do I. Desperately . . . !" She felt his tongue and the edge of his teeth as he moved over the warm expanse of her shoulders and her collarbone in a silence blazing with promise.

His breath sounded oddly jerky as he drew her body against him. "You taste like the sweetest kind of candy," he said under his breath, and his fingers were hurting, but she was too shaken to care. "Baby," he whispered, his mouth growing urgent now as it found her throat, the underside of her chin. His hands moved up to catch in her hair, careless of its neat bun, as he bent her head back and lifted it toward his hard, parted lips. "Baby, you make me ache . . . !"

His mouth was poised just above hers, and at that moment she'd have given him that and anything else he wanted. But before he could lower his head, the sound of a door being opened shattered the hot silence.

"Oh, damn," Egan ground out. His fingers bruised her, and his eyes were blazing as he pushed her away and turned as if he were blinded by his own passion—a frustrated passion like that which was making her tremble.

"Marshal's sick of the sea, but they won't let him come home," Ada sighed, oblivious to the wild undercurrents around her. "Why couldn't I find myself a man instead of a sailor? Ili, Kati. Have a good time?"

"Sure," Kati said, smiling through a haze of unsatisfied longing. She glanced toward

Egan and saw his eyes, and she flushed wildly. Her eyes went to his mouth and back up; and he muttered something terrible under his breath and slammed into his room without even the pretense of courtesy.

"What's the matter with him?" Ada asked softly.

"Beats me," her friend replied blandly. "Gosh, I'm tired. We went dancing and my feet are killing me!"

"Well, I hope you don't wear them out before Friday night," Ada laughed. "Sleep well."

"I'll do my best," came the muttered reply, and she went into her room and almost collapsed. He hadn't even kissed her, and she was trembling like a leaf. Heaven only knew what would happen if he ever really made a heavy pass. She couldn't bear to think about it! She went to bed and lay awake half the night brooding, only to wake with a splitting headache the next morning.

Egan brooded all day. He moved restlessly around the apartment, like a man aching for the outdoors. Even Kati felt vaguely sorry for him.

"You'll wear ruts in the carpet," she murmured after lunch, while Ada was taking her turn at the dishcs.

He turned with his hands rammed deep in his pockets and stared at her. "If I do, I'll buy you a new one."

"That wasn't what I meant," she said, trying hard to hold on to her temper. She searched his hard face, but she couldn't quite meet his eyes. "You hate being indoors, don't you?"

"With a passion," he agreed shortly. "I couldn't live like this."

"New York is full of things to see," she suggested. "There's Central Park, and the Statue of Liberty, the Empire State Building—"

"I've already seen them once," he said. "And I've walked the streets. What I want, I'm not going to find out there."

She lifted her eyes and had them trapped.

He moved closer so quickly that she hardly saw him coming before he was towering over her. "I want you," he said, his voice like warm velvet in the sudden silence of the room. "I'm through pretending."

"Well, I don't . . . I don't want you," she said in a breathless little voice. "I have a boyfriend—"

"No competition whatsoever," he returned. "What are you afraid of? I'm not brutal in bed. I wouldn't hurt you."

She flushed deeply, and just stopped herself from slapping him. "I liked it better when you hated me," she said angrily, glaring up at him.

His eyes searched hers. "Was it ever that?"

Her lips parted, but before she could find an answer, Ada was through with the dishes and Kati stuck to her like glue until it was time to leave for dinner that evening.

Jack grinned as he saw Kati in her burgundy velvet dress. "What a dish," he murmured. "And I like your hair down like that."

"Thank you. You aren't bad yourself. Jack, you know Marshal," she said, indicating the tall, dark young man beside Ada.

"Sure." Jack extended his hand. "Good to see you again."

"Same here," Marshal replied. He hugged Ada close. "I still love the sea, but sometimes I get a little hungry for the shore."

"I can imagine. Uh, wasn't your brother supposed to join us?" Jack asked Ada with evident reluctance.

"He's meeting us at the Rainbow Grill," Ada said. "And I made reservations in advance."

"Good girl," Jack said. He took Kati's arm. "Well, let's get it over with," he murmured under his breath.

"It will be all right," she promised as Ada and Marshal fell back. "We can have the waiter pour wine over his head if he starts anything."

"You don't think he would?" Jack asked, horrified.

She patted his arm. He wasn't the type for public scenes, although Kati wouldn't have minded dousing Egan any old where at all. "No, I don't," she promised. "Don't worry. Everything will be fine."

She was to remember those words vividly a little later, when Egan joined them at their table overlooking the colorful lights of the city sixty-five floors down. He had on his arm a windblown little blonde who looked and dressed like a woman who loved money, and her first glance at the other women was like a declaration of war.

"So this is Ada," the blonde gushed, heading straight for Kati.

"Wrong woman," Kati said shortly. "That's Ada."

The blonde shrugged, gave a careless smile and turned to greet a highly amused Ada. "So you're Ada. How nice to meet you at last. I've just heard so much about you from Egan. We've known each other for a long time, you know. He calls me every time he gets to New York. I'm a model."

As if that didn't stick out a mile, Kati thought as the blonde sat down near her and almost choked her with expensive perfume.

"Isn't this the most gorgeous place?" the blonde enthused. "I love the atmosphere. And isn't the combo great?"

Kati couldn't say. She hadn't been able to hear them play, or hear their sultry-voiced vocalist sing, for the newcomer. And just as she was wondering how she'd eat because of the perfume, Egan slid into the seat beside her and ruined her appetite completely.

"Jennie Winn, this is Katriane James and her date," Egan volunteered.

Kati glared at him. "Jack Asher," she supplied.

"Nice to meet you, I'm sure," Jennie murmured. "What do you do, Mr. Asher?" she asked Jack and batted her impossibly long eyelashes at him.

He perked up immediately, the turncoat. "I'm a political columnist, for the *Times*," he said.

Jennie beamed. "Are you, really? Oh, I just adore intelligent men."

Kati had to muffle a giggle with her napkin. Really, she was behaving impossibly, but that blonde couldn't be for real!

"Something amuses you, Miss James?" Egan asked with ice in his tone.

She got herself under control. "I got strangled, Mr. Winthrop," she managed.

"On what? The air?"

"Now, Egan, honey," Jennie crooned, glaring past him at Kati. "You just relax, and later I'll take you back to my place and soothe you."

Kati bit almost through her lip to keep from howling. She didn't dare look at Egan—it would have been the very end.

"Jennie, look at the menu," Egan said curtly.

"Whatever you say, sugar."

"I want the beef Wellington," Ada said. "How about you, Kati?"

"Do they serve goose here?" Egan asked under his breath.

"If they do," Kati replied with a venomous smile, "yours is probably sizzling on the grill right now, sugar."

He glared at her and she glared back at him. Sensing disaster, Jack quickly intervened.

"Kati, didn't you want to try that duckling in orange sauce?"

She tore her eyes away from Egan's and smiled across the table. "Yes, I did."

By then the waiter was back, elegant in his white jacket, to take their order. By and large, Kati loved New York waiters. They had a certain flair and grace of manner that set them apart, and they were unfailingly polite and kind.

"I want prime rib," Jennie said nonchalantly. "Rare, honey."

"A woman after my own heart," Egan murmured. "I'll have the same."

Kati wanted to mutter something about barbarism, but she kept her mouth shut with an effort. And when the food came, she was far too involved in savoring every morsel to waste time on Egan Winthrop.

But the coffee and dessert came, eventually, and while Kati toyed with her superb English trifle, Egan leaned back and eyed Jack.

"I read your column on the Washington scandal," he told the younger man.

"Did you?" Jack asked with a polite smile.

"Interesting, about the deficit in the agency's budget," he continued. "Apparently your man was allocating funds on paper that never reached the recipients. The audacity of politicians constantly amazes me, and so does the apathy of the public."

Jack perked up. "Yes. What I can't understand is how he expected to get away with it," he said, forgetting his dessert as he went into the subject.

Egan matched him, thought for thought, and the ensuing conversation fascinated Kati. She listened raptly, along with everyone else at the table except Jennie—who looked frankly bored to death.

"You know a hell of a lot about politics for a rancher, Mr. Winthrop," Jack said finally, on a laugh.

"I took my degree in political science," came the cool reply. "Ranching pretty much chose me, rather than the other way around. When my father died, there was Ada and my mother to look after, and no one else to assume control of the property. There was a lot of it.'' He shrugged. ''The challenge is still there,'' he added with a smile. ''Cattle are a lot like politics, Mr. Asher. Unpredictable, hard to manage and sometimes just plain damned frustrating.''

Jack laughed. ''I imagine so.''

''Oh, can't we stop talking about such boring things?'' Jennie asked in a long-suffering tone. ''I want to go to the theater, and we've got tickets to that hit musical on Broadway. We'll be late if you talk all night.''

Egan gave her a look that would have stopped traffic.

Jennie flushed and cleared her throat. ''I mean, whenever you're ready, sugar,'' she said placatingly.

Kati lifted her chin with faint animosity. She'd have told him where to go, instead of pleading with him like that. He knew it, too. Because he glanced at her and caught the belligerent gleam in her eye, and something wild and heady flashed between them when he smiled at her.

Her lips trembled, and she grabbed her coffee cup like a shield.

"See you later," Egan told them, picking up the tabs. "My treat. I enjoyed the discussion," he told Jack.

Before anyone could thank him, he and Jennie were gone and Jack was shaking his head.

"And I thought he hated me. My God, what a mind. He's wasted out West."

Ada beamed. "He was offered an ambassadorship, did you know?" she asked. "He knows everybody in Washington, right to the top. But he turned it down because of mother and me. Since then, he's given everything to the ranch."

"Not quite everything," Marshal murmured. "His girl was a knockout."

"I'd have liked to knock her out," Kati muttered, flushing at Ada's shocked look. "Well, she must have bathed in perfume; I could hardly breathe," she said defensively.

But Ada only grinned, and Kati hated that knowing look. So she was jealous! She caught her breath. She was jealous? Of

Egan? She picked up the untouched wine-glass and helped herself.

Egan wasn't home when they finally got back to the apartment, and Kati could just picture him with that sizzling blonde. It made her ache in the oddest way. She took a shower and got ready for bed and then paced and paced around her room.

"Is something bothering you?" Ada asked minutes later, coming in to check on her. It wasn't like Kati to pace. "You're getting to be as bad as Egan about wearing ruts in the carpets."

Kati lifted her shoulders helplessly, grabbing at the ribbon strap that kept sliding off. The green gown was far too big, but she liked its roominess. "I'm just restless."

Ada studied her friend quietly. "He's a man," she said softly.

Kati blushed all the way down her throat and turned away.

"I'm sorry, I shouldn't have said that," Ada said hesitantly. "But, you see, I can't help noticing the way you look at him. And the way he looks back. Normal people don't fight like the two of you do. Anything that explosive has to... well, there has to be something pretty powerful to cause it, don't you see?''

"I hate him," Kati said through her teeth. "That's powerful, all right."

"But you want him."

Kati's eyes closed. "Tomorrow is Christmas," she said. "The day after, he'll go back to Wyoming and I'll go back to my sordid books, and we'll both be better off. There's no future with your brother for any woman, Ada, and you know it.'' She turned around, her face stiff with control. "He's not the happily-ever-after kind."

Ada looked worried. "He says that, but no man really wants to get married, does he? It kind of takes the right woman."

Kati laughed huskily. "A woman like Jennie. She suits him just fine, doesn't she?" she asked venomously.

Ada shook her head. "She numbs the hurt, that's all. He's a lonely man."

"He got hurt once and never wants to be again, is that how it goes?" Kati asked.

"I don't think Egan can be hurt, Kati," came the soft reply. "He doesn't let anyone close enough. I know less than nothing about his private life. But I think he's more involved with you right now than he's ever been before."

"He's never touched me," she bit off.

"Yes, I know. I didn't mean physically," Ada said. "I mean emotionally. Don't you realize that's why he hits at you so hard?"

"He hits at me because he wants me," she told the other woman bluntly. "He said so. He thinks I'm easy."

Ada looked horrified. "Well, did you tell him the truth?"

"Of course not! I don't owe your horrible brother any explanations— Let him just keep his disgusting image of me!"

Ada frowned slightly. "Kati, he isn't a man to let go of something he sets his mind on. I think you'd better tell him."

"Why bother? He'll be gone day after tomorrow," she repeated.

"Kati—"

"Go to bed and stop worrying about me," Kati said gently, and hugged her concerned friend. "Egan and I will go on being enemies, because I won't give in and he'll give up. He makes a nice enemy."

"You wouldn't think so if he'd ever really been yours," Ada replied.

"Anyway, we both need our sleep. It will all work out, somehow. Sleep well."

Ada gave up. She smiled as she went out. "You, too."

But Kati didn't. Not until the wee hours of the morning. And Egan still hadn't come home. He was with that blonde, kissing her with that wide, cruel mouth that had tormented hers so sweetly....

Something woke her. She didn't know what. But she felt the light on her eyelids and the coolness of air on her skin, and her dark, drowsy eyes opened slowly.

He was standing beside the bed, wearing nothing but a pair of slacks, with his broad chest sensuously bare and a cup of black coffee in one hand. And he was looking at her in a way that brought her instantly alert

and wary; his glittering silver eyes were on
fire.

She frowned slightly as she realized that he
wasn't looking at her face. Her eyes shifted,
and she noticed to her embarrassment that
the loose gown had shifted in the night,
leaving one perfect breast pink and bare.

Her hand went to jerk the bodice back up.

"No, Kati," he said in a husky undertone, and his eyes went back up to hers.
"No. Let it happen."

He moved close, setting the coffee on the
table. He dropped smoothly down beside
her, and she hated the sudden weakness and
hunger of her body as she stared up at him.
Her hair was spread out on the pillow like a
ragged halo of red and gold, her cheeks rosy
with sleep, her eyes sultry. And he looked
just as disheveled, just as attractive to her,
with his hair tousled, his muscular arms and
chest bare and tanned.

His hands went under her head, both of
them, and he eased down so that his chest
rested on her partially bare one.

She gasped at the unfamiliar sensation of skin on skin, and her eyes dilated under the piercing scrutiny of his.

"I'm going to kiss you until you can't stand up," he said roughly, bending. "My God, I want your mouth...!"

He took it, with a hard, hungry pressure that frightened her. Her slender hands lifted quickly to his shoulders and started to push—until they discovered the rough silkiness of his skin, the power in his bunched muscles. She ran her hands slowly down his arms, feeling the tension of the hard muscles, and back up again, to the hard bone of his shoulders.

Meanwhile, his mouth was slowing, gentling. He lifted it so that it was poised just over hers, and he looked at her for a long moment.

"You don't like it hard, do you?" he asked in a gruff undertone. "I do. Hard and hot and deep. But I'll make the effort, at least."

He bent again, coaxing her lips. It was an education in sensual blackmail. She lay tense under the crush of his torso, feeling each brief, soft contact like a brand. Her lips parted because she couldn't stop them, her breath was coming in short gasps and her heartbeat was shaking her. She hadn't known that women felt like this, despite the novels that bore her name. All her research had come from books, from films and television and bits and pieces of gossip. But what Egan was teaching her bore no resemblance to any of that. He was making her catch fire, and she was moving and reacting in ways that embarrassed her.

"That's more like it, baby," he breathed. "Much, much more like it. Now," he whispered, letting his hands slide down the long, bare line of her back, "now, if you want my mouth, come up and get it."

Blind, aching, she arched up and caught his hard mouth with hers, kissing him with enough enthusiasm to make up for her lack of experience at this kind of impassioned caress.

She felt his tongue go into her mouth, and she moaned sharply at the intimacy.

He lifted his dark head as if the sound had shocked him, and looked down at her rigid, anguished features. His free hand tugged slowly at the other strap of her gown and his eyes followed its movement.

"Do you want me, Kati?" he asked quietly. "Shall I get up and lock the door?"

Her mind cleared instantly with the words as she stared up into his blazing eyes. He was asking her a straightforward question, and the answer would have been an unqualified *yes*. But he was offering a quick, temporary merging of bodies that would shame her when her sanity returned. And what in heaven's name would Ada think?

As if he sensed the indecision, his hand stilled on her arm. "Second thoughts?" he asked softly.

"I...can't," she whispered, searching his narrow eyes.

"I understand," he murmured, glancing toward the door with a wry smile. "We're not likely to be alone much longer."

He thought it was because of Ada, and it didn't really matter, did it? Whatever the reason, the result was going to be the same.

He looked back down at her and shifted so that the thick hair on his chest rubbed against her soft bareness; he smiled at her reaction.

"Like it?" he murmured arrogantly, and his hand came up to tease the softness under her arm, making her gasp.

"You have to stop that," she told him in a halting tone.

"Do I?" He bent and brushed his mouth lightly over hers while his fingers toyed with the silken skin and edged slowly, relentlessly, toward the hardening nub that would tell him graphically how he was affecting her.

"Egan?" she whispered in a voice that sounded nothing like her own. Her fingers lifted, catching in his hair, and her body was no longer part of her. It was his, all his, and every inch of it was telling him so.

His nose rubbed against hers as his mouth brushed and lifted; and his fingers made nonsense of principles and morals and self-respect.

"Kati?" he whispered, sensuously. He nipped at her lower lip. "Kati, take my hand and put it where you want it."

It was the most wildly erotic thing she'd ever heard or dreamed or thought. Helplessly, she reached out for his hand and carried it to the aching peak, and pressed it there.

"Oh God," she ground out, trembling, her face pressing into his hot throat, her body shuddering with the force of her own hunger.

"Silk," he whispered, his own voice rough and unsteady. "You're silk. So soft, so whisper-soft." His mouth found hers and he kissed her so tenderly that tears welled in her eyes, while his hand cupped and his thumb caressed, and it was the sweetest ache in the world that he caused her.

And then, all at once, the bodice was back in place, the sheet was over her and she was lying, shaking, in the bed as he propped up pillows and set her against them like a big doll.

"Ada," he ground out, handing her the cup with hands that trembled.

Her own trembled, and between them they just got it steady as Ada opened the door without knocking and came in yawning.

"Morning," she murmured, grinning at them. "I've got breakfast. Bring your coffee with you. Thanks for taking it to her, Egan."

"My pleasure," he murmured, and went out without a backward glance.

"Bad mood again?" Ada grimaced. "I thought it might mellow him up if I sent him in with your coffee. I guess I goofed again. Well, hurry up and dress, I've got something special!" Ada added and went out the door laughing.

Kati sat there with tears suddenly rolling down her cheeks, so shaken and frustrated that she wanted to scream the roof down. She should have listened to Ada, she told

herself. Ada had known what she didn't—
that Egan was relentless when he wanted
something. And what he wanted now was
Kati.

Chapter Six

Ada had made fresh croissants—so light and flaky they could almost fly—and she had real butter to go on them. But Kati didn't taste anything she ate. She felt as if she were in the throes of some terrible fever, and every time she glanced at Egan, it got worse.

He was wearing a shirt and his boots now, with his dark slacks, and he was still beautiful. Kati could hardly drag her eyes away.

"You must have been late last night," Ada

remarked to her brother. "I didn't hear you come in."

"I let myself be talked into going to a party after the show," he muttered. "Damned bunch of freaks. It was like a drugstore in there."

"You left," Ada said with certainty.

"I left. And took Jennie with me. And she screamed bloody murder all the way back to her apartment." He laughed shortly. "Which got her nowhere at all. She knew how I felt about that from the beginning, I never made any secret of it."

"Things are different in the city, Egan," Ada said sadly. "Very different."

His head lifted. "Geography doesn't change what's right and what isn't," he said shortly.

"I know that," Ada agreed. "I don't like it any more than you do, but I don't feel I have the right to dictate to the rest of the world. Kati and I just keep to ourselves."

He glanced at Kati then, his eyes sweeping over her pale jersey blouse and slacks possessively. "Are you an old-fashioned girl in that respect, at least?'' he asked, but he didn't sound so sarcastic as usual. ''Do you drink and pop pills and smoke pot?''

''I drink cola,'' she replied. ''And I do take aspirin when my head hurts.'' She watched him with wide eyes. ''But I don't think I've ever tried to smoke a pot. What kind of pot did you have in mind?''

He burst out laughing. It changed his entire face, erased some of the hard, leathery lines. He looked faintly attractive, despite that cragginess. ''My, my, aren't we sharp this morning?''

She lowered her eyes before he could read the embarrassment in them. ''Eating improves my mind.''

''I know something better,'' he remarked just as she lifted the coffee cup to her mouth.

''Don't move!'' Ada gasped as hot coffee went all over the table and into Kati's lap. ''I'll get a towel!''

She disappeared, and Egan mopped at her legs with a napkin.

"That was damned poor timing on my part," he muttered. "I didn't mean to make you hurt yourself."

She looked up into his silver eyes, astonished. "That's a first," she breathed.

He looked back, his gaze intent. The napkin rested on her thigh. "Did I tell you how lovely you are?" he asked under his breath. "Or what it did to me to touch you like that?"

She felt her lips part helplessly. "Egan, about... what happened—"

"I want it again," he breathed, bending so that his mouth threatened hers. "I want you against me so close that I can feel your heart beating."

"You don't understand," she whispered weakly.

"You want me," he returned huskily. "That's all I need to understand."

It was true, but it wasn't that uncomplicated. And before she could tell him how complicated it really was, Ada was back and the moment was lost. And she was trembling again.

She walked around like a zombie, going through the motions of helping Ada in the kitchen. They invited Marshal and Jack over for dinner the next day, since neither of them was going to try to go home for Christmas. And getting everything ready was a job.

Egan watched television and paced. Finally he got his jacket and hat and went out, and Kati almost collapsed with relief. She ached every time she looked at him, until it was torment to be within seeing distance.

He came in just as the annual Christmas Eve specials were beginning on the public broadcasting station, and he tossed his hat onto the hall table and shed his jacket.

"Culture," he murmured, watching the opera company perform.

"Go ahead, Mr. Winthrop, make some snide remark," Kati dared, feeling young and full of life because her heart leaped up just at the sight of him.

He smiled at her, with no malice at all on his dark face. "I like opera."

"You?"

"Well, there was a report awhile back on music and milk production," he told her, dropping easily into his armchair, "and it seems that cows produce more milk when they're listening to classical music."

Kati smiled. "It must cost a lot."

"What?"

"Having the orchestra come all the way out to the ranch."

"You little torment," he accused and reached out to tug a lock of her long hair playfully.

Ada, watching all this, just stared at them.

"Something wrong?" Egan asked her.

Ada shrugged. "Not a thing in this world, big brother."

He grinned at her. "Where's your boyfriend?"

"Begging for liberty on his knees," she told Egan. She laughed. "If he gets it he'll be here any minute."

"I'd bet on him." He glanced at Kati. "How about yours?" he asked tautly.

"Jack's making calls to his family," she said. "He won't be over until tomorrow."

He didn't say anything, but he settled down in the chair to watch the programs with an oddly satisfied smile.

Marshal came a few minutes later, and Egan even joined in when they sang Christmas carols during the next program. They drank eggnog and ate cake, and Kati thought she'd never been so happy in her life.

Ada led Marshal under the mistletoe on his way out at midnight and kissed him lovingly, winking at Kati as the two of them moved out into the hallway.

"I'm going to walk Marshal to the elevator," she called back. "Don't wait up."

"Don't fall down the elevator shaft!" Kati called after her.

The door closed on a giggle. Which left Kati alone with Egan and trembling with new and frightening emotions.

He stood up, holding out his hand. She put hers into it unhesitatingly and let him lead her to the mistletoe. His lean, strong hands caught her waist and brought her gently against the length of his hard body.

"I've waited all day for this," he whispered, bending.

She stiffened, but his hands smoothed down over her hips and back and he nudged his face against hers gently.

"I know how you like it, baby," he breathed. "I won't hurt you this time, all right?"

She was beyond answering him. Her body throbbed. Throbbed! It was the most incredible physical reaction she'd ever had in her life, and she couldn't control it.

His mouth opened and hers opened to meet it, inviting the new intimacy, and she drowned in the magic of the long, sweet kiss. She breathed him, the tangy fragrance of cologne and, closer, the minty hotness of his mouth.

"I want you," he whispered, his voice shaking.

She drew back a little, trying to catch her breath and regain her sanity. It was impossible, but she couldn't even speak. They were simply torturing each other with this kind of thing. But how could she explain it to him?

He rested his forehead on hers and his eyes closed on ragged breaths. Against her hips, his body was making an embarrassing statement about his feelings, and she withdrew just enough to satisfy her modesty.

"Still playing games, Kati? You don't have to put on any acts for me. That virginal withdrawal—"

"Egan, you have to listen to me," she managed, looking up.

"I've got an apartment two streets over," he said on a harsh breath. "One even Ada doesn't know about. We could be there in fifteen minutes, and she'd never have to know."

Her breath caught in her throat. His eyes were blazing with it, and she knew her own legs were trembling. For one wild second she looked up at him and knew how it would be between them. She could almost feel the length of him without clothes: the silken slide of skin on skin, the aching pleasure of being touched by those lean, expert hands...

"Come with me, Kati," he said unsteadily. "We're just torturing each other. I've got to have you."

"I can't," she ground out. She lowered her chin so that her tormented eyes were on a level with his chest, and her trembling fingers pressed against his warm shirt.

His fingers tautened on her waist, moved to her hips and jerked them into his. "I ache," he whispered. "You know what I'm feeling."

Her eyes closed. She wasn't stupid; she could imagine that it was ten times worse for him than it was for her. But she couldn't undo all the years of conditioning. Flings weren't for her. She had too much conscience.

"I'm sorry," she whispered. "I'm so sorry, Egan, but I can't."

He drew in an angry breath, and she stiffened because she knew he was going to go right through the ceiling. She couldn't even blame him; she should never have let him touch her.

But oddly enough, he didn't say a word. He loosened his grip on her hips, allowing her to move away, and drew her gently into his arms. He held her, his head bending over her, his heartbeat shaking both of them, until his breathing was normal again.

Her hands felt the warm strength of his back even through his shirt, and she loved the protected feeling she got from being close like this. Her eyes closed and, just for a moment, she allowed herself the luxury of giving in completely, of pretending that he loved her.

"I could make you," he whispered at her ear. "I could take the choice away."

"Yes, I know," she agreed softly. Her cheek nuzzled against his chest.

"This kind of passion is a gift," he said quietly. "I could give you pleasure in ways you've never had it with another man. Not because I'm any damned prize in bed, but because we react to each other like dynamite going up."

"I can't," she replied softly. "I want to, but I can't."

His hand smoothed her long hair gently. "Because of him?"

She drew in a steadying breath. She was going to have to tell him, and it wasn't going to be easy.

The door opened, thank God, and Ada walked in, stopping dead when she saw the two of them wrapped in each other's arms.

"Wrestling match?" she guessed. "Who's winning?"

"Mistletoe," Egan murmured, nodding upward. "Damned potent stuff. She's got me on my knees."

"That'll be the day," Ada grinned.

Kati pulled away, and he let her go with obvious reluctance. "And I didn't poison you, either," she murmured, trying to keep it light.

"Didn't you?" he returned, but there was a difference in him now, a strangeness.

"No fighting," Ada said. "It's Christmas day."

"So it is," Egan said. "Where's my present?"

"Not until morning," Ada returned.

"Damn." He looked down at Kati. "I like presents. What did you get me?"

"Not until morning," she echoed Ada.

He lifted an eyebrow. "I hate waiting," he murmured, and only Kati knew what he meant.

"All good things come to him who waits, though," Ada interrupted; and then wondered why Kati blushed and Egan laughed.

The girls went in to bed, but Kati didn't sleep. She wanted Egan. And there was more to it than that. She was beginning to feel something she'd never expected. She thought ahead to the next day, when he'd leave for Wyoming, and the world went black. She couldn't imagine a day going by without the sight of him. Just the sight of him.

She sat straight up in bed and stared at the wall. She hadn't known that it could happen so quickly. Of course, it could be just physical attraction. She did want him very much, and it was the first time she'd wanted any man. She knew nothing about him really, except bits and pieces. So how, she asked herself, could she be in love with him?

"Love," she whispered out loud. She licked her dry lips and put it into words. "I...love...Egan." The sound of it made tingles all the way to her toes, and when she closed her eyes she could feel his mouth on hers; she could taste the minty warmth of his lips. Shivers went all over her like silvery caresses, and she caught her breath.

You have to forget all that, she told herself. Because what Egan wanted was the limited use of her body, to sate his own hunger. And once he'd had it, he'd be off to new conquests. Like Jennie. Her eyes clouded with bridled fury. Jennie! She'd like to rip the girl's hair out.

She lay back down and closed her eyes. Well, that was his kind of woman, anyway. All she had to do was grit her teeth and bear it until he left. Then she could pull her stupid self together and forget him. Her eyes opened. It was over an hour before she could close them in sleep.

Chapter Seven

The thought of the condominium bothered Kati. She couldn't help remembering that Egan had said Ada didn't know about it, which meant he kept it for only one reason. If he was willing to take Kati there, he must have taken other women too. In the cold light of morning, she was glad she'd had the sense to resist him. Egan only wanted her. Someday, with a little luck, there would be a man who'd love her.

But if she was inclined to be cool and collected, Egan wasn't. He watched her covetously when she joined them for breakfast. His silver eyes roamed over the pretty red vest and skirt she was wearing with a long-sleeved white blouse, and he smiled appreciatively.

"Very Christmasy," he murmured.

She smiled as coolly as possible. "Thank you."

She allowed him to seat her, expecting Ada to plop down beside her as usual. But instead, Egan slid into Ada's usual place, so close that his thigh touched hers when he moved.

"I can help," Kati volunteered quickly.

"No," Ada said as she dished up everything and carried it to the table. "Just sit. We'll both have enough to do later."

So she sat, nervously, hating the close contact because she could feel Egan as well as smell the warm, manly fragrance of his body. He was dressed up, too, in a navy pin-stripe suit that made him look suave and sophisticated. And all the time she picked at her bacon and eggs, he watched her. It was as if he were launching a campaign, with her as the objective. And it was getting off to a rousing start.

Ada noticed the tension and smiled. Kati flushed at that smile, because she knew her friend's mind so well.

It didn't help that Ada finished early and announced that she just had to have a shower before she dressed.

"Afraid to be alone with me?" Egan teased gently when the door closed behind his sister.

"Oh yes," she admitted, looking up with fascinated eyes.

His own eyes seemed unusually kind and soft, and he smiled. "Why?" he asked. "Because of last night?"

She lowered her eyes to his smooth chin, his chiseled mouth. She remembered the feel of it with startling clarity.

"Don't hide." He tilted her face back up to his and studied it quietly. "I can wait. At least, until you've had time to break it off with Asher."

So that was what he thought! That was why he'd been so patient last night. He assumed that she was sleeping with Jack and had to end the affair before . . .

She caught her breath. "But I can't—"

"Yes, you can," he said. "Just tell him how it is. He doesn't seem to be so unreasonable to me. In fact—" he laughed shortly "—he hardly touches you in public. A man who's committed to a woman usually shows a little more warmth."

"I don't like that kind of thing, around people," she murmured.

"Neither do I, for God's sake," he bit off. "But when people get involved, it happens sometimes. A look, a way of touching, a hand that can't let go of another hand— there are signs. You and Asher don't show them."

"He's . . . very reserved," she returned.

"So are you. Even alone with me." He leaned closer and brushed his mouth over hers like a breath. "Ada won't be gone that long. And then we'll be surrounded by people. And I won't be able to do this to you. . . ."

His hand contracted behind her head, catching her hair, tangling in its fiery depths

HOW TO VALIDATE
YOUR
EDITOR'S FREE GIFT
"THANK YOU"

1. Peel off gift seal from front cover. Place it in space provided at right. This automatically entitles you to receive four free books and a beautiful Porcelain Trinket Box.

2. Send back this card and you'll get brand-new Silhouette Romance™ novels. These books have a cover price of $2.99 each, but they are yours to keep absolutely free.

3. There's no catch. You're under no obligation to buy anything. We charge nothing—ZERO—for your first shipment. And you don't have to make any minimum number of purchases—not even one!

4. The fact is thousands of readers enjoy receiving books by mail from the Silhouette Reader Service™ months before they're available in stores. They like the convenience of home delivery and they love our discount prices!

5. We hope that after receiving your free books you'll want to remain a subscriber. But the choice is yours—to continue or cancel, anytime at all! So why not take us up on our invitation, with no risk of any kind. You'll be glad you did!

6. Don't forget to detach your FREE BOOKMARK. And remember...just for validating your Editor's Free Gift Offer, we'll send you FIVE MORE gifts, *ABSOLUTELY FREE!*

YOURS FREE!

*This beautiful porcelain box is topped with a lovely bouquet of porcelain flowers, perfect for holding rings, pins or other precious trinkets — and is yours **absolutely free** when you accept our no risk offer!*

THE EDITOR'S "THANK YOU" FREE GIFTS INCLUDE:

▶ Four BRAND-NEW romance novels
▶ A Porcelain Trinket Box

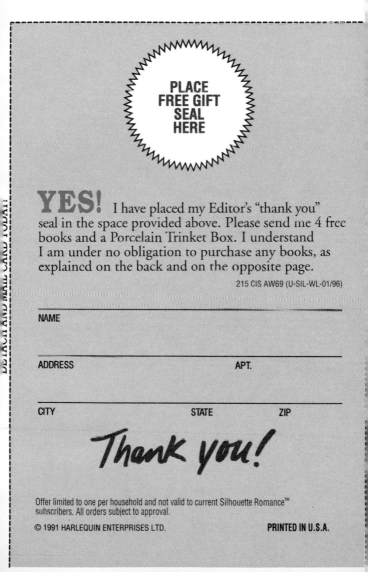

```
PLACE
FREE GIFT
SEAL
HERE
```

YES! I have placed my Editor's "thank you" seal in the space provided above. Please send me 4 free books and a Porcelain Trinket Box. I understand I am under no obligation to purchase any books, as explained on the back and on the opposite page.

215 CIS AW69 (U-SIL-WL-01/96)

NAME

ADDRESS   APT.

CITY   STATE   ZIP

Thank you!

THE SILHOUETTE READER SERVICE™: HERE'S HOW IT WORKS

Accepting free books places you under no obligation to buy anything. You may keep the books and gift and return the shipping statement marked "cancel". If you do not cancel, about a month later we will send you 6 additional novels, and bill you just $2.44 each plus 25¢ delivery and applicable sales tax, if any.* That's the complete price, and—compared to cover prices of $2.99 each—quite a bargain! You may cancel at any time, but if you choose to continue, every month we'll send you 6 more books, which you may either purchase at the discount price...or return at our expense and cancel your subscription.

*Terms and prices subject to change without notice. Sales tax applicable in N.Y.

to press her mouth to his. As if passion were riding him hard, he bit at her closed lips and shocked them into parting. And then she was his. Totally his, as he explored the soft warmth of her mouth expertly, possessively.

When he stopped, her hands were clenched in his thick hair, and she moaned when he lifted his mouth.

"No more, baby," he whispered huskily. "We don't have the luxury of privacy, and I had a hard enough time sleeping last night as it was. A man can only stand so much."

Her eyes opened slowly and she looked up at him drowning in the silver of his eyes. "I didn't mean to tease," she whispered. "It wasn't like that."

"I know that," he replied quietly. "You were with me every step of the way, from the first second I touched you. Circumstances have been the problem. I need to be alone with you. Completely alone." He drew in a slow breath. "Come back to Wyoming with me, Kati."

Her eyes dilated. "What?"

"You said you had to research that damned book. All right. I'll help you. Fly out with me in the morning, and I'll show you everything you need to know about ranch management."

She studied his hard face. She knew exactly what he was saying: "during the day." His eyes were telling her that he had different plans for the night, and she already knew exactly what *they* were.

"Still afraid?" he asked thoughtfully, watching the expressions change on her young face. "Let's get it out in the open. Why? Do I strike you as a brutal man? Do you think I'd be kinky in bed or something?"

Her face burned and she looked down. "I've never thought about it."

"Liar. You've thought about it every second since yesterday morning, just like I have." He bent his head and kissed her quickly, roughly. "It was just the way I told you it would be. We touched each other and exploded. I wanted you, and it made me rough at first. But it won't be that way anymore. I promise you, Kati. I'll be as tender a lover as you could want.''

"You...you never seemed gentle," she said involuntarily. "And you've been so harsh with me...."

He brushed a lock of hair back from her cheek and frowned as he looked down at her. "It's the way you write, damn it," he said. "So...openly."

"Egan, I don't make love with strange men in bathtubs," she said. It was one of the ironies of her life that she could write torrid romances at all. But the writing never embarrassed her. It was as if the characters did what they wanted to, taking over as the words went onto paper. The situations arose from the characterizations, not out of her own personal experience.

He shrugged. "That may be. But no man likes to think he's being used for research."

Her eyes opened wide. Her eyebrows went straight up. "You don't imagine that I...that I'd even consider—" She felt herself puffing up with indignation. "Oh, you monster!"

She jerked up from the table, glaring down at him as she fought tears of pure fury. "What do you think I am, damn you, an exhibitionist? What I write comes out of nowhere! The characters create themselves on paper, and their own motivations produce the love scenes! I do not write from personal experiences with a multitude of lovers!"

"Now, Kati," he began, rising slowly.

"But you just go on thinking whatever you please, Egan," she continued. "You just go right ahead. I don't care. I don't need you at all!"

And she turned, tears in her eyes, and ran from the room, colliding with Ada.

"Hey, what's the matter?" Ada asked gently.

"Ask Dracula!" came the broken reply, and she threw a last accusing glare at Egan before she went into her room and slammed the door.

It was a bad start for the day. And it didn't help that when she got herself together and came back out, Egan had vanished. She'd overreacted, and she was ashamed. But his opinion of her had hurt in unexpected ways and brought home how he considered her widely experienced.

Wouldn't he be shocked, she thought miserably, to know how innocent she was?

In fact, the love scenes in her books were mild compared to those in other genres. They were sensuous, but hardly explicit. That was why she was able to write them. She didn't have to go into a lot of explanations that she'd have to dig out of anatomy books anyway—because she didn't know the first thing about fulfillment, except what she'd learned second-hand.

"Will he be back?" Kati asked miserably when Ada told her that Egan had walked out.

Ada lifted her shoulders helplessly. "I don't know. Things were going so well this morning. What happened?"

"He accused me of doing my own research for the love scenes," she muttered. "In bathtubs with strange men." She hid her face in her hands. "You can't imagine how it hurt to have him think so little of me!"

"Then why not tell him the truth, my dumb friend?" Ada asked. "He doesn't read minds, you know."

"Because . . ." She clenched her fists and hit the air impotently. "Because," her voice lowered, "the only thing about me that attracts him at all is my 'experience.'"

Ada gaped at her. "You're in love with him," she said half under her breath.

Kati smiled sadly. "Doesn't it show? Hasn't it always shown? Ada, I'd walk over a gas fire just to look at him."

"And I thought you hated him."

"I did. Because he hated me, and I knew it would never be more than that." She smoothed her hair. "And now it's worse, because he's like a bulldozer and I'm terrified of him."

"I warned you," Ada reminded her. "He's utterly relentless."

"He wants me to go home with him," she said.

Ada's face brightened. "He does?"

"Don't be silly, I can't go! If I do, he's bound to find out what an absolute idiot I am, and then where will I be? He'll throw me out on my ear!"

"And then again, he might not."

"I'm no gambler, Ada. Losing matters too much. I'd rather stay here and pull the pieces together. Maybe it's just a physical infatuation and I'll outgrow it," she added hopefully.

"If you'd walk through fire just to look at him, darling," Ada said gently, "it's got to be more than physical. And you know it."

"But what can I do?" Kati wailed. "Ada, I'm not the kind to have affairs. I'm too inhibited."

"Not when you write, you aren't!"

"That's different. When I write, I'm a storyteller, telling a story. In real life, I get too emotionally involved, and then I can't let go. And Egan hates even the idea of involvement."

"He looked pretty involved to me this morning. He could hardly take his eyes off you long enough to eat," Ada remarked.

"You know why, too."

"Men are attracted first; then their emotions get involved. Look at Marshal and me! He liked my legs, so he called me. And now here we are almost engaged!"

"And here it is Christmas and I've ruined it again," Kati moaned.

"No, you haven't. Egan will be back when he cools down. He's mad at himself, I'll bet, not at you." She smiled. "He didn't mean to hurt you."

Tears welled up in her eyes and she turned away. "I never meant to hurt him, either."

"Then cheer up. It will all work out, honest it will."

"So you keep saying. I'll try to listen this time."

They had everything ready just as Marshal and Jack arrived, and the four of them stood around and talked until noon.

"Should we wait for Egan?" Marshal asked.

"Well," Ada said, biting her lower lip. "I don't know when he'll be back."

Even as she said the words, the front door opened and Egan walked in. He tossed his Stetson onto the hall table.

"Waiting for me? I got held up at Jennie's," he added, glancing toward Kati with pure malice in his eyes.

So much for Ada's helpful optimism, Kati thought as she took off her apron. She didn't even look at him again, and her entire attitude was so cool and controlled that she felt she deserved an Oscar for her performance all the way through the holiday meal. The turkey was perfectly browned, the ham beautifully glazed. Egan, at the head of the table, carved, and Ada passed the plates down. He said grace, and everyone was far too busy to talk for the first few minutes.

Kati was just bursting with fury about Jennie. She could imagine what Egan had been doing and why he'd been held up. She was rigid with the effort not to get up and fling the turkey carcass the length of the table at him.

"The cherry pie is delicious," Jack offered as he finished his last mouthful and followed it with the rich black coffee Ada had made.

"Thank you," Kati said with a smile.

"Kati does all the desserts," Ada told Marshal. "I'm no hand at pastry."

Egan hadn't touched any of the pies or fruitcake. He barely seemed to eat anything, like Kati. Her eyes found his across the room, and it was like lightning striking. She felt the longing she'd been fighting down all day coming to life again. It was incredible that she could look at him and go to pieces like this.

"Well, I hate to eat and run," Jack said, "but I promised my cousin I'd stop by and see him and his family this afternoon. There are so few of us left these days."

"Yes, I know what you mean," Ada said quietly, and her face showed the loneliness Kati knew she must feel this first Christmas without her mother.

"I'm sure you do. I'm sorry, I didn't mean to bring up such a sad subject," Jack apologized.

Ada smiled. "Don't be silly. Happy Christmas, Jack. I'm glad you could come."

"Me, too," Kati said, avoiding Egan's eyes as she got up to walk Jack to the door.

"I enjoyed it," Jack said. "Merry Christmas!"

Kati saw him out into the corridor. "I'll see you later, then."

Jack stared down at her quietly. "Do you realize how that big cattleman feels about you?" he asked unexpectedly.

Her face paled. "What?"

"He watched you as if he'd bleed to death looking. And the one time I smiled at you, I thought he was going to come over that table to get me." He laughed self-consciously. "If you get a minute, how about telling him that we haven't got anything serious going? I'd like to keep my insurance premiums where they are."

She laughed too, because they were friends who could ask such things of each other. "I'll do my best. Want to spend New Year's with us?"

"As far as I know, I don't have a thing planned. But," he added with a wink, "you might. So let's leave it alone for now, and I'll call you. All right?"

"All right. Merry Christmas," she added.

"You, too." He bent and kissed her lightly on the cheek. He was just lifting his head when Egan appeared in the doorway with eyes that glittered dangerously.

"You're taking a long time just to say good-bye," he muttered.

"Discussing the weather," Jack said quickly. "Damned cold outside! In here, too. Bye, Kati!" And he took off for the elevator with a grin.

Egan caught Kati's hand in his, holding it warmly, closely, and pulled her just inside the door. They were out of view of the living room, and when he closed the outside door, they might have been alone in the world.

"I can't stand it," he ground out, gripping her arms as if he were afraid she'd fly out of his reach. "You're driving me out of my mind, damn it!"

"You started it," she bit off, keeping her voice down.

"I didn't mean it, though," he returned in a harsh undertone. His hands loosened their grip, became caressing, burning her even through the blouse's long sleeves. "Kati, I'm so used to hitting at you . . . but this morning I didn't mean to."

Her lower lip trembled as she looked up at him. "You went to her," she said shakily.

Every trace of expression left his face, and only his eyes showed any emotion at all. They glittered at her like silver in sunlight. "I didn't touch her," he said huskily. "How could I? All I want in the world is you!"

Her lips parted, and before she could speak, he bent and caressed them slowly, sensuously, with his own. His breath was suddenly ragged, uneven, and the hands that were on her arms moved up to cup her face and hold it where he wanted it.

"Are you going to fight me every inch of the way?" he asked in a strained tone.

"I'm not," she protested dazedly.

"Then kiss me," he murmured.

She didn't understand what he meant until the pressure of his mouth forced hers open and she felt his tongue in a slow, even penetration that made her blood surge.

She gasped, and he deepened the kiss even more. She felt his body tremble, and he groaned softly—deep in his throat—like a man trying to control the impossible. He whispered her name under his breath and his arms went around her like chains. He crushed her into the taut muscles of his body until she hurt, and she didn't care. She wanted to be closer than this, even closer, with nothing in the way...!

"Kati?" Ada called from the living room.

In a fever of hunger, Kati watched Egan lift his head and take a slow, steadying breath.

"We're talking, all right?" he asked in what sounded like an almost normal tone.

"Oh, excuse me!" Ada called back. "Never mind!"

Egan's eyes burned down into Kati's. "Are you all right?" he whispered, watching the tears shimmer in her eyes.

"Yes. I...just...just feel kind of shaky," she stammered.

He took her hands to his hard chest and held them over the vest. "So do I," he said. "From the neck down. My God, you stir me up!"

Her eyes searched his slowly, curiously. "You're a passionate man," she whispered. "I imagine most women make you feel that way."

He shook his head very slowly. "I'm not promiscuous, Kati. I'm selective. It takes a very special woman."

She felt unreasonably flattered, but then, she wasn't thinking straight. How could she, this close to him, wanting him with a fever that was burning her alive?

"I'm scandalous, remember?" she said. "I seduce men to help me with my research—"

He stopped the words with a touch to her lips. "I'm not a virgin. How can I sit in judgment on you?"

"If you'd listen to me," she said softly, "I'd tell you."

"I don't want to hear it," he said curtly. "The past is over. We'll go from here. Are you coming home with me?"

And there was the question she'd wanted and dreaded, staring her in the face. She looked at him and knew she wasn't going to be strong and sensible. She could feel herself falling apart already.

"You won't...expect too much?" she asked hesitantly.

"Listen," he said, brushing his fingers over her warm cheek, "as far as I'm concerned, you're coming to learn about ranching for a book. You don't have to pay for your keep, Kati. In any way," he emphasized. "I'll let you come to me. I won't ask more than you want to give."

She lowered her eyes to his vest and wondered again, for the hundredth time, what it would be like with him—and knew that it was suicide to think about it.

"Come home with me," he said, tilting her face up to his. "The snow's sitting like a blanket on the Tetons, and the river's running through it like a silver thread. I'll show you where the buffalo used to graze and the mountain men camped.''

He made it sound wildly romantic, and his eyes promised much more than a guided tour. It was crazy! She was crazy!

"I'll go home with you, Egan," she whispered.

His breath caught and he studied her eyes for a long moment before he bent to kiss her softly, slowly on her swollen lips. "There's a bear rug in front of the fireplace in my den," he breathed at her lips. "I've wondered...for years...how it would feel on bare skin, Kati."

A tiny, wild sound escaped from her throat, and he lifted her in his arms to kiss her roughly, possessively, until the whole world compressed into Egan's mouth and arms.

"Er-ahmmmm!" came a loud noise from the doorway.

Egan drew away with shaky reluctance and let Kati slide back to her feet just as Ada peeked around the corner.

"Marshal and I wondered if you'd like to go walking and look at the city," Ada asked, trying not to look as pleased as she felt.

"I'd like that," Egan said, smiling down into Kati's rapt face. "Would you?"

"Yes," she said dreamily.

"I hope you don't mind living alone for a couple of weeks, Ada," Egan added as he grabbed his hat and topcoat. "Because I'm taking Kati to Wyoming."

"You are?" Ada burst out, her face delighted.

"To help her with the book," he added, glaring at his sister. "Research, period."

"Oh, of course," Ada said, getting a firm grip on herself. "What else?"

Kati didn't dare look up. It would have blown her cool cover to pieces. Then Egan caught her small hand in his big one as they went to the elevator, and every thought in her head exploded in pleasure. Her fingers clung, locking into his. She walked beside him feeling as if she owned the world, oblivious to the beauty of New York City in holiday dress. Her present was right beside her.

It was almost dark when they came back to the apartment, after looking in store windows and eyeing the decorations around Madison and Fifth Avenues. Then they exchanged presents, and Kati was overwhelmed when she opened Egan's gift. It was a silver bracelet—pure silver with inlaid turquoise, and surely not a trinket. She looked up, pleasure beaming from her dark eyes, to thank him.

"Do you like it?" he said on a smile. "I like mine too."

She'd given him a new spinning reel, something Ada said he'd appreciate. Although, at the time, pleasing Egan hadn't been on Kati's list of priorities, now she was glad she'd bought it. She saw the real appreciation in his eyes.

All too soon it was bedtime, and Ada was seeing Marshal out in a protracted good night.

"You'll have to get up early," Egan told Kati as they said their own good night at the door of her room. "I want to be out of here by eight."

She smiled. "I'll pack tonight. I have to bring my computer."

"One of those portable ones with a built-in telephone modem?" he asked knowledgeably.

She nodded. "It's my lifeline. I can't manage without it. It even has a printer built in."

"I carry one with me when I travel," he said. "We inventory our herds on computers these days, and use them to print out the production records for sales. I even sell off cattle by videotape. Ranching has moved into the twentieth century."

"I'll feel right at home," she said, laughing.

"I hope so," he said, his face softening as he looked down at her. "No strings, baby. I won't back you into any corners."

She nodded. "Sleep well."

"Without you?" he murmured wistfully. "No chance."

He bent and kissed her lightly. "Night."

And he was gone.

She walked into her room and closed the door, feeling impossibly happy and terrified all at the same time. What was going to happen when, inevitably, Egan discovered that her reason for going wasn't his reason for inviting her? Because things were bound to come to a head. And either way, he'd discover for himself that she wasn't the worldly woman he thought her. What would he do? She shuddered. He'd probably be furious enough to put her on the first plane to New York.

She reached for the doorknob. She almost went to tell him that she'd changed her mind. But the prospect of even a few days alone with him—to glory in his company— was like the prospect of heaven. And she was too besotted to give it up. Just a day, she promised herself. Just one day, and she'd confess everything and let him do his worst. But she had to have that precious time with him. It would last her all her life. It would be all she'd ever have of him.

Chapter Eight

Her first sight of the Tetons as she and Egan flew over Jackson Hole made Kati catch her breath.

Seated beside Egan in the ranch's small jet, she stared down at the velvety white tops of the jagged peaks with wonder.

"Oh, it's beautiful," she whispered. "The most beautiful thing I've ever seen!"

"You've never been here in the winter, have you?" he asked, smiling. "I'd forgotten. Honey, if you think this is something, wait until I get you on the Snake."

"Snake?" Her ears perked up and she looked at him apprehensively.

"River," he added. "From the ranch house, we overlook the Snake, and the Tetons look like they're sitting over us."

"I knew it was spectacular in the spring and summer," she sighed, staring back out the window. "But this is magic."

He watched her with quiet, smiling eyes. "I was born here, but it still sets me on my heels when I come home. A lot of battles have been fought over this land. By Shoshone and Arapaho and the white man, by ranchers and sheepmen and rustlers."

She glanced at him. "Are there still rustlers out West?"

"Of course, but now they work with trucks. We have a pretty good security system, though, so we don't lose many. Feeding the cattle during the winters is our biggest problem," he said. "We're pretty fanatical about haying out here, to get enough winter feed. A cow won't paw her way through the snow to get food, Kati. She'll stand there and starve first."

"I didn't know that," she said, fascinated.

"You've got a lot to learn, city lady," he said with a soft laugh. "But I'll teach you."

That, she thought, was what she feared. But she only smiled and watched the familiar lines of the big two-story white frame house come into view as they headed for the landing strip beyond it.

"How old is the house, Egan?" Kati asked after Egan had told the pilot to take the jet to the Jackson airport where it was based.

"Oh, I guess around eighty or ninety years," he said. He led her to a waiting pickup truck. "My grandfather built it."

"And called it White Lodge?" she asked, remembering that the ranch also was called by that name.

"No. That was my grandmother's idea. She was Shoshone," he added with a smile.

She studied him quietly. "And your grandfather? Was he dark?"

He nodded. "The sun burns us brown. Despite all the damned paperwork, I still spend a lot of time on horseback."

"Hi, Boss!" Ramey yelled out the window of the pickup truck.

"Hi, Ramey!" Egan called back. He opened the door and put Kati inside, jerking a thumb at Ramey to get him out from behind the wheel.

"I ain't such a bad driver," Ramey grumbled.

"I don't care what kind of driver you are," Egan reminded him as he got in next to Kati and shut the door. "Nobody drives me except me."

"On account of Larry ran him into a tree," Ramey explained as he shut his own door just before Egan started down the snowy ranch road. The young boy grinned at Egan's thunderous look. "Broke Larry's nose."

"Hitting the tree?" Kati asked innocently.

"Hitting the boss's fist afterward," Ramey chuckled.

Kati glanced at Egan. "And I thought you were the sweetest-tempered man I'd ever met," she said dryly.

Ramey's eyebrows arched. He started to speak, but Egan looked at him and that was all it took.

"Don't reckon you got a Chinook tucked in your bag somewheres?" Ramey asked instead, his blue eyes twinkling.

"A what?" Kati asked blankly.

"Chinook," Egan said. "It's a warm wind we get here in the winter. Melts the snow and gives us some relief." He looked over her head at Ramey. "How's the feed holding out?"

"Just fine. We'll make it, Gig says. Gig is our foreman," Ramey reminded her. "Kind of came with the ranch, if you know what I mean. Nobody knows how old he is, and nobody's keen to ask him."

"The answer might scare us," Egan chuckled. "Damn, this stuff is deep!"

He was running in the ruts Ramey had made coming to the landing strip, but it was

still slow, hard going, and powdery snow
was beginning to blow again.

"It'd be faster if we walked," Ramey
suggested.

"Or rode." He shot a quick glance at
Kati, letting his eyes run over her beige dress
and high heels and short man-made fur coat.
"God, wouldn't you look right at home on
horseback in that? I almost made you
change before we left Ada's."

She started to object to the wording and
then let it go. Why start trouble?

"No comeback?" Egan chided. "No remarks about my tyrannical personality?"

"Why, Mr. Winthrop, I'm the very soul of
tact," she said haughtily.

"Especially when you're telling me to go
to hell," was the lightning comeback.

She flushed, noticing Ramey's puzzled
look.

"We, uh, sometimes have our, uh, little
differences," she tried to explain.

"Yes, ma'am, I recall," Ramey murmured, and she remembered that he'd been

nearby when she had walked furiously off the ranch that summer.

She cleared her throat. "Well, you do have the Tetons at your back door, don't you?" she asked Egan, who seemed to be enjoying her discomfort.

He followed her gaze to the high peaks rising behind the house. "Indeed we do. And the river within sight of the front door," he added, indicating the winding silver ribbon of the Snake that cut through the valley far below the house.

"Elk and moose and antelope graze out there during the winter," he told her. "And buffalo used to, in frontier days."

"I've never seen a moose," she said.

"Maybe this time," he told her.

She watched as Egan's elderly housekeeper waddled onto the front porch, shading her eyes against the blinding white of the snow. Egan left the truck idling for Ramey and lifted Kati off the seat and into his hard arms. The sheepskin coat he wore made him seem twice as broad across the chest and shoulders.

"You're hardly equipped for walking in the snow," he murmured, indicating her high heels. "I hope you packed some sensible things."

"Hiking boots, jeans and sweaters," she said smartly.

"Good girl. Hold on."

She clung as he strode easily through the high blanket of snow and up onto the steps, his boots echoing even through the snow against the hard wood. Dessie Teal was watching with a grin, her broad face all smiles under her brown eyes and salt-and-pepper hair.

"I never would have believed it," she muttered as Egan set Kati back on her feet. "And I don't see a bruise on either one of you."

"We don't fight all the time," Egan said coolly.

"Well, neither do them Arabs, Egan," Dessie returned, "but I was just remarking how nice it was that you and Miss James seemed to be in a state of temporary truce, that's all."

"She came to research a book about Wyoming in the old days," Egan told the old woman gruffly, his eyes daring her to make anything else of it.

Dessie shrugged. "Whatever you want to call it. A book about frontier days, huh?" she asked, leading Kati into the house. "Well, you just go talk to Gig, he'll tell you more than any book will. His daddy fought in the Johnson County range war."

Kati asked what that had been about and was treated to fifteen minutes of Wyoming history, including references to the range wars between cattlemen and sheepmen, and the ferocity of Wyoming winters.

"My brother froze to death working cattle one winter," Dessie added later, when Kati had changed into jeans, boots and a sweater and was drinking coffee with the housekeeper in the kitchen. "He fell and broke his leg and couldn't get up again. He was solid ice when one of the men found him." She shivered delicately. "This ain't the place for tenderfeet, I'll tell you." She paused in the act of putting a big roast into the oven. "How come you and Egan ain't fighting?"

"He's trying to get me into bed," Kati returned bluntly and grinned wickedly at the housekeeper's blush.

"I deserved that," Dessie muttered and burst into laughter. "I sure did. Ask a foolish question . . . Well, I might as well make it worse. Is he going to?"

Kati shook her head slowly. "Not my kind of life," she said. "I'm too old-fashioned."

"Good for you," Dessie said vehemently. "Honest to God, I don't know what's got into girls these days. Why, we used to go two or three dates before we'd hold hands with a boy. Nowadays, it's into bed on the first one. And they wonder why nobody's happy. You gorge yourself on candy and you don't want it no more. At least, that's how I see it."

"You and I should join a missionary society," Kati told her. "We don't belong in the modern world."

Dessie grinned at her. "Well, speaking for myself, I ain't in it. Can't get much more primitive than this, I reckon, despite all the modern gadgets Egan bought me for the kitchen.''

"I understand what you mean." She leaned back in the chair and sipped her coffee. "Did Egan really not want to be a rancher?" she asked.

Dessie measured that question before she answered it. "I don't think he knew exactly what he did want. Politics used to fascinate him. But then, so did business. And that's mostly what ranching is these days; it's business. He has Gig to look after the practical side of it while he buys and sells cattle and concentrates on herd improvement and diversification." She grinned sheepishly. "What big words!"

"Is he happy?" Kati asked, because it mattered.

"No," Dessie said quietly. "He's got nobody except Miss Ada."

Kati studied her coffee cup, amazed at how deeply that hurt her. "He's...not handsome, but he has a way with him. And he attracts women," she added, remembering Jennie.

"Not the right kind of women," came the tart reply. "Not ever one he could bring to this ranch. Until now."

Kati blushed to the roots of her hair.

"Now what are you doing?" Egan growled from the doorway, taking in Kati's red face and Dessie's shocked expression at his sudden appearance. "Talking about me behind my back, I guess?"

"Well, who else is there to talk about?" Dessie threw up her hands. "I never see anybody except you. Well, there's Ramey, of course, but he don't do nothing interesting enough to gossip about, does he?"

Egan shook his head on a tired sigh. "I guess not. Damn. You and your logical arguments." He took off his hat and coat. "What's for dinner? I'm half-starved."

"You're always half-starved. There's some sliced turkey in the refrigerator, left over from my solitary Christmas dinner I had all by myself, alone, yesterday."

Egan glanced at the old woman. "Did you have a good time?" he asked.

"I told you I ate by myself!" Dessie growled.

"Well, I guess that means you didn't have any company," Egan said pleasantly.

"Wait," the housekeeper said, "until tonight. And see what I feed you for supper."

"Let me die of starvation, then," he said. "I'll call up Ada and tell her you won't feed me, and see what you do then!"

Dessie threw down her apron. "Hard case," she accused, her lower lips thrusting out. "Just hit me in my weakest spot, why don't you?"

Egan grinned, winking at Kati, who was seeing a side of him she hadn't dreamed existed. She liked this big, laughing man who seemed so at home in the wilderness.

He even looked different from the man in the pinstripe suit in Ada's apartment. He was wearing denim now, from head to foot, and a pair of disreputable brown boots that had seen better days— along with a hat that was surely obsolete. The only relatively new piece of apparel he had was the sheepskin coat he'd just taken off. But he seemed bigger and tougher and in every way more appealing than the sophisticated executive.

"You look different," Kati remarked absently, watching him.

He cocked an eyebrow as he carried turkey and mayonnaise to the table. "I do?"

"His looks ain't improved," Dessie argued.

"Just mind your own business, thank you," he drawled in her direction and watched her go back to her roast. "And don't burn that thing up like you did the last one!"

"I didn't burn nothing up," she shot back. "That stupid dog of yours got in here and reared up on my stove and changed the heat setting!"

"Durango doesn't get in the house," he told her. "And he isn't smart enough to work a stove, despite being the best cattle dog I own."

"Well, I wouldn't turn my back on him," she muttered. She put the roast in the oven and closed the door. "Excuse me. I got to go to the cellar and get apples. I thought you might like an apple pie. Not that you deserve one," she added, glaring back as she went out the door.

He only laughed. "Get the bread, honey, and I'll make you one too," he told Kati.

"Where is it?"

"In the breadbox."

She got up and went to the cabinet to get it, but before she could turn around, he was behind her, the length of his body threatening and warm.

"Fell right into the trap, didn't you?" he breathed, turning her so that her back was against the wall. With his hands on the wall beside her, he eased down so that his body pressed wholly on hers, in a contact that made the blood surge into her face.

"God, it's wild like this, isn't it?" he said unsteadily. "I can feel you burning like a brand under every inch of me."

She opened her lips to speak, and he bent and took them. His mouth was cold from the outdoors, but hers warmed it, so that seconds later it was blazing with heat. A

moan growled out of his throat into her
hungry, wanting mouth.

She felt his tongue, and her eyes opened
suddenly, finding his closed, his brows
drawn, as he savored the pleasure. But as if
he felt her looking at him, the thick lashes
moved up and his darkening silver eyes
looked straight into hers.

On a caught breath he lifted his lips just
fractionally over hers. "Now, that's excit-
ing," he whispered. "I've never watched a
woman while I kissed her."

But obviously he was going to, because his
eyes stayed open when he bent again, and so
did hers. The hunger and need in his kiss in-
flamed her, and her hands found their way
to the top button on his shirt.

She'd never wanted to touch a man's bare
skin. She couldn't remember a time in her
life when the thought had appealed. But it
did now. She could feel the crush of his hips
and thighs over hers, and explosive sensations were curling her toes.

Her fingers toyed with his top button
while she tried to decide how risky it would

be. He was hungry enough without being tempted further, and she wasn't sure she could handle him.

He lifted his head and watched her fingers. "Are you always this unsure of yourself with a man?" he asked under his breath. "Or is it just me? Touch me if you want to, Kati. I won't lose my head and bend you back over the kitchen table."

The wording made it sound cheap, made her sound cheap. The color went out of her face and she eased away from him.

He swore quietly, watching her get the bread and some saucers and start making sandwiches in a strained silence.

"What do you want from me?" he ground out.

She drew in a steadying breath. "I'd settle for a little respect. Not much. Just what you'd give any stranger who came into your house." Tears welled in her eyes as she spread mayonnaise. "I'm not a tramp, Egan Winthrop."

He watched a solitary tear land with a splatter on the clean tabletop, and his hands caught her waist convulsively, jerking her back against him.

"Don't...cry," he bit off, his fingers hurting.

"Don't touch me!" she threw back, twisting away from him.

He held onto the edge of the table, glaring as she wiped the tears away and finished making the sandwiches. She pushed his at him and went to put the knife in the sink.

He poured coffee into her cup and his, put the pot away and sat down. She followed suit, but she ate in silence, not even looking at him. Fool, she told herself. You stupid fool, you had to come with him!

Dessie came back to a grinding silence. She stared at them, apples in her apron, and grimaced. "I leave you alone five minutes and you start a war."

Egan finished his coffee and got up, not rising to the bait. "I've got work to do."

He grabbed his coat and hat and stamped out the door. Kati brushed away more tears. Dessie just shook her head and started peeling apples. After a minute, she got another bowl and knife and pushed them at Kati.

"Might as well peel," she told her. "It'll give your hands something to do while your mind works."

"Mine doesn't work," Kati replied coldly. "If it did, I'd still be in New York."

"Not many people get under his skin like that," Dessie commented with a slow grin. "Good to know he's still human."

"Well, I'd need proof," Kati glowered.

"I think you'll get it," came the laughing reply. "Now, peel, if you want an apple pie."

Kati gave in. And it *was* rather soothing, peeling apples. She had a feeling she was going to make a lot of pies before she got her research done.

Chapter Nine

After that little episode, Egan became remote. He was the perfect host, polite and courteous, but about as warm as one of the rocks on his land.

Kati decided that if he could play it cool, so could she. So she was equally polite. And distant. Oddly enough, there were no more violent arguments like the ones they had in the past. Once in a while, she'd notice Egan watching her over the supper table before he disappeared into his study to work, or during a rare minute in the morning before he went to his office down the road. But he kept to himself, and the affectionate, hungry man who'd brought her to the ranch seemed to have vanished into his former, cold counterpart.

But she did accomplish one of her goals. She learned enough about ranching to do a nonfiction work on it.

The logistics of supplies fascinated her. Egan's cows and second-year heifers were bred to drop calves in February and March. So during January, the ranch manager and his men were very much involved in precalving planning. That meant buying ear tags, identifying first-calf heifers, checking breeding dates to estimate calving dates and arranging for adequate facilities.

Because of the increased herd, move calving pens had to be added, but those were erected during the fall. The cowboys were closely watching the cows now to make sure there were no problems. One of the older hands told her that he always hated being a cowboy during this time of the year and at roundup in the spring, when the cattle had to be branded, vetted, and moved about fifty miles away to summer pasture.

Listening to the men tell about their adventures took up the better part of her days. She was careful not to interfere with their work, having been cautioned by the boss about that. But she was around during breaks and sometimes after dinner, with her pad and pen in hand, asking questions.

It would have been all right if Ramey hadn't asked her to go to a dance with him. Egan happened to overhear the question, and before Kati could even get her mouth open to say "No, thanks," Egan was on top of them.

"If you're through irritating the men," he told her cuttingly, "they need their rest."

She rose, embarrassed to tears but too proud to show it. "Excuse me, I didn't realize—"

"But, boss," Ramey groaned, "she wasn't bothering us!"

There was a loud tumult as the other cowboys in the bunkhouse agreed with pathetic eagerness.

"All the same, good night," Egan said in his coldest tone. He held the door open; Kati, seeing defeat, shrugged, calling a smiling good night to the men and walked knee-deep in the melting snow back to the truck she'd commandeered for the drive down.

"This way," Egan said curtly, taking her arm. He led her to his pickup truck and put her inside.

"I was just asking questions," she muttered. "You told me not to interfere with their work."

"I didn't say you could sleep with them," he growled.

"You pig!" she burst out. Her eyes blazed; her lips trembled with fury. "How dare you accuse me of such a thing!"

"Ramey asked you out—did you think I didn't hear him?" he asked. He fumbled for a cigarette, surprising her, because she'd seen him smoke only once or twice in the past few days.

"I was going to refuse," she replied. "He's a nice boy, but—"

"But not experienced enough for a woman like you, right?" he asked, smiling insolently.

Her breath stopped. "What exactly do you mean, 'a woman like me'?" she asked deliberately.

"What do you think I mean?"

She clutched the pen and pad in her hand and stared straight ahead.

"No comeback?"

"I won't need one. I'm going home."

"Like hell you are."

"What do you plan to do, Mr. Winthrop, tie me up in a line cabin?"

"Who taught you about line cabins?"

"Gig," she said uncomfortably, remembering the long, amusing talk she'd had with the sly old foreman.

"Gig never talks to anybody, not even me."

"Well, he talks to me," she shot back. "But I guess you'll accuse me of trying to get him into bed too!"

"You'd hate it," he said, lifting the cigarette to his mouth. "He only bathes once a month."

She tried to keep her temper blazing, but she lost and hid the muffled laugh in her hands.

He glanced at her, his eyes sparkling. "If I stop making objectionable remarks to you," he said after a minute, "do you suppose we might try to get along for the duration?"

"I don't think that's possible," she said, glancing at him. "You won't even give me the benefit of a doubt."

"I've read your books," he reminded her.

"How in God's name do you think Edgar Rice Burroughs wrote *Tarzan of the Apes?*" she exploded. "Do you believe that he swung from trees in darkest Africa? When he wrote the first book, he'd never even seen Africa!"

He pulled up at the front door and cut off the engine. "Are you trying to tell me that a woman could write a sexy book without having had sex?'' He laughed. ''No dice, baby. I'm not stupid.''

''That depends on your definitions,'' she returned hotly. ''About me, yes, sir, you are stupid.''

''Only when you kiss me in that slow, hot way,'' he murmured, smiling wickedly, ''and try to take off my shirt.''

She slammed the pen against the pad impotently and glared at him.

''All right,'' he said after a minute and crushed out the cigarette. ''I'll apologize for the crude remark I made in the kitchen. Will that pacify you?''

''I want to make something crystal-clear,'' she returned, gripping the pad tightly. ''As far as I'm concerned, I'm here to research a book.''

His eyes darkened and he studied her closely. ''Put it in words, not innuendos.''

''I don't want to be mauled around,'' she replied.

''Tell Ramey. He was the one who wanted to take you off into the woods,'' he said on a laugh.

"So did you!" she accused.

He shook his head. "No. I wanted to take you into my bed. There's a difference."

"Geographical," she countered.

He sighed and reached out to smooth a long, unruly strand of her hair. "I want you. I haven't made any secret of it. You want me, too. It's just going to take more time than I thought."

"I won't sleep with you," she told him.

"You will," he replied softly, searching her eyes. "Eventually."

"Is that a threat?" she asked, finding her fighting feet.

"No, ma'am," he said, grinning.

She glared at him uncertainly. "I don't understand you."

"You've got a whole lot of company," he told her. He dropped her hair. "Better get some rest. And don't go back to the bunkhouse at night. Keeps the boys awake."

"I have to find out some things about calving," she protested.

"Do you? What do you want to know?" he asked with a wicked smile.

"Oh, stuff your hat . . . !" she began.

"Now, now, you mustn't shock me," he told her as he got out of the truck. "I'm just an unsophisticated country boy, you know."

"Like hell," she muttered under her breath.

He opened her door and lifted her into his arms. She started to struggle, but he held her implacably and shook his head.

"Don't fight," he said. "We've spent days avoiding each other. I just want to hold you."

She felt a rush of feeling that should have made her run screaming the other way. But instead, she put her arms—pad and pen and all—around his neck and let him carry her. By the time he got to the steps, her face was buried in his warm throat and her heartbeat was shaking her.

"We haven't made love since we were in New York," he whispered as he carried her into his study and deliberately locked the door behind him.

She felt her lips go dry as she looked up at him. He was taking off his hat and coat, and the way he was staring at her made her feel threatened.

"No more games, Katriane," he said softly. He took away the pad and pen, and, bending, took off her warm coat and dropped it beside his on the chair. He lifted her off the floor. "I won't hurt you. But I've gone hungry too long."

There would never be a better time to tell him the truth. But just as she started to, he bent and pressed his open mouth against the peak of her breast. She cried out, shocked speechless at the intimacy of it even through two layers of cloth.

He didn't say a word. She felt him lower her, felt the soft pile of a rug under her back. And then his body was spreading over hers like a heavy blanket, making fires that blazed up and burned in exquisite torment.

His mouth moved up to hers, taking it with a power and masculine possessiveness that she'd never felt before. She wasn't even aware of what his hands were doing until he lifted her and she felt the slight chill of the room and the heat of the blazing fire in the hearth on her bare flesh.

"Egan," she protested shakily as he laid her back down.

"God, you're something!" he breathed, looking down with wild, glittering eyes on what he'd uncovered. His hands went to the buttons on his shirt and unfastened them slowly, methodically. He pulled the shirt free of his jeans and stripped it off, revealing bronzed skin that shimmered smoothly in the light of the fire.

Her eyes fastened on him hungrily, loving every rugged line of him, wanting the feel of his hard muscles against her own trembling softness.

There was only the crackle of the fire as they looked at each other, only its reddish glow in the room. She knew what he was going to do, but she was powerless to stop him. She loved him. Oh God, she loved him!

He came down slowly, easing his chest over hers by levering himself over her on his arms. His eyes held hers every second as he brushed his chest against her taut breasts and watched the wild, sweet surge of her body upward to make the contact even closer.

"Don't hold anything back with me," he said under his breath. "And I'll please you until you scream with it."

His mouth eased down as his chest did, and she reached up to catch his head in her hands, tangle her fingers in his hair while he kissed the breath from her swollen mouth.

She experienced her own power when she felt the tremor in his long body; and without thinking about consequences, she tugged his head up and shifted to bring his lips down to the bareness of her body.

"Kati!" he burst out as if she'd surprised him, and he dug his hands in under her back. His mouth opened, and she felt his tongue, his teeth at flesh that had never even known a man's eyes.

Her body rippled in his arms, on waves of sweetness, and she moaned as his mouth learned every smooth inch of her above the waist. He rolled suddenly onto his back, bringing her with him, and she felt his hands going under the waistband of her jeans onto the softness of her lower spine.

"Look at me," he said in a husky tone.

She lifted her head just as his clean, strong hands contracted, and he smiled at the hunger he could read in her eyes.

He nipped her earlobe with his teeth and whispered things that excited and shocked, all at once, embarrassing things that she'd only read until that moment.

"Egan," she protested weakly.

"Just relax," he whispered, bringing her hips back against his in a slow, sweet rotation. "Let me show you how much I want you."

He ground her hips into the powerful, taut muscles of his own. She cried out as he freed one hand to bring her shaking mouth down onto his, thrusting his tongue up into it in a rhythm that said more than words.

"My room," he whispered. "Right now."

He rolled her over and handed her the blouse and sweater he had taken off her minutes before. "You'd better put those on," he said in a taut undertone. "In case Dessie's still up."

She clutched the cool things to her, staring at him like someone coming out of a trance.

"Well?" he ground out. "My God, you felt what you've done to me. I need you, damn it!"

She swallowed, trying to find the right words. "I need you too, Egan," she said shakily. "But there's something you'd... you'd better know first."

"What? That you aren't on the pill?" he demanded. "It's all right, I'll take care of it. I won't let you get pregnant."

She blushed and lowered her eyes to the jerky rise and fall of his chest. Her fingers tightened on the shirt and sweater. "I'm a virgin."

"My God, that's a good one." He laughed coldly. "Try again."

"I don't have to," she said, trying to hold on to her pride and her self-respect, both of which were slipping. "I've told you the truth."

"Sure, I'm a virgin, too," he told her. "Now can we go to bed?"

"Go right ahead," she said with venom in her tone. "But without me! Didn't you hear what I said, damn you, I'm a virgin!"

"At twenty-five?" he asked in a biting tone. "Writing the kind of books you write?"

"I've told you until I'm blue in the face that I don't research those love scenes—most of which are foreplay with a hint of fulfillment!" She flushed, avoiding his eyes. "And some of that is obligatory; I can't get historical fiction published without it. And as for men . . ." she added, lifting her face to glare at him, "most of them have felt as you do, that a woman's place in the modern world is to be available for sex and then disappear before anyone gets emotional. I can't live like that, so I don't indulge."

"Never?" he burst out.

"Never!" she returned. "Egan, didn't Ada ever tell you about my parents?"

His breathing was steadier now, but he still looked frustrated and full of venom. "That they were old?"

She took another steadying breath of her own. "My father was a Presbyterian minister," she whispered. "And my mother had been a missionary. Now do you understand?"

He looked as if he'd been slapped. His eyes went over her, right down to the fingers that trembled on her discarded top. "Why didn't you tell me?" he ground out. "My God, the things I said to you...!"

He got to his feet and grabbed up his shirt, shouldering angrily into it. "Get out of here," he said coldly.

She managed to get to her feet gracefully, pausing as she tried to decide between running for it and dressing first.

"Put on your blouse, for heaven's sake!" he snapped, and turned away again to light a cigarette with jerky motions.

She put on the blouse and pulled the sweater on over it without ever fastening a button. She couldn't even look at him as she walked toward the door. Her fingers fumbled with the lock, and when she pulled the door open, he still hadn't turned or said a word. She closed it quietly behind her with trembling fingers and went upstairs as quickly as she could. When she was safely in her room, with her own door locked, she burst into tears.

Chapter Ten

It was the most agonizing night Kati remembered spending. Egan had bruised her emotions in ways she hadn't dreamed possible. Rejecting her was enough of a blow. But couldn't he have done it gently? She cringed, thinking of the way he'd been, the things he'd said until she confessed. Ada had warned her. Why hadn't she listened?

Worst of all was the fact that she'd been more than ready to give in to anything he wanted of her. She'd wanted him to know the truth because he was so hungry that she was afraid of being hurt the first time. But her revelation had backfired. Instead of comforting her, he ordered her out of the room and turned his back.

Well, at least she knew how he really felt now, she told herself miserably. She knew that he'd only wanted her, and there was no feeling on his part except desire. She couldn't remember ever hurting so much. She loved him. What she'd felt in his hard, expert embrace was something she'd never get over. But he'd turned away as if such devastating interludes were just run-of-the-mill. To him, they probably were. With good-time girls like Jennie.

She got up well before daylight. She packed quickly and dressed in her boots and jeans and a burgundy sweater. She decided to go downstairs and have breakfast, and make sure Egan had left the house before she called a cab. It was eight o'clock, and he was usually long gone by then. She didn't know how she could face him if he was still there, not after last night. It made her color, just

remembering the things they'd done together.

Her footsteps slowed as she reached the
kitchen. She pushed the door open part way
and found Dessie puttering around the stove.
With a sigh of relief, she pushed it open the
rest of the way and came face to face with
Egan, who was just behind it picking up his
hat from the counter.

She actually jumped aside. He looked
down at her with an expression she couldn't
read. His eyes were dark silver, cold, angry.

"I want to talk to you for a minute," he
said curtly.

He didn't give her a chance to protest. He
propelled her through the door and down the
hall to the living room. He shut the door behind them and stared hard at her.

"Before you start," she said in a painfully subdued tone, "I realize it was all my
fault, and I'm sorry."

He pulled a cigarette from his pocket and
lit it, his fingers steady. "We won't talk
about last night," he said. "Stay the week

out, finish your research. If you run off this morning, you'll just upset Dessie and Ada.''

''What do you mean, if I run off?'' she countered defensively.

''Aren't your bags packed already?'' he asked, lifting his head at an arrogant angle.

Damn his perception, she thought furiously, turning her eyes to the curtained windows. ''Yes,'' she snapped.

''Then unpack them. You came here, obviously, for a different reason than I brought you,'' he said with the old, familiar mockery. ''Since your work is obviously so important, by all means indulge yourself. Just stay out of the bunkhouse after dark. We've got a couple of new men that I don't know well.''

''The only people I really need to talk to are Gig and Ramey,'' she told him with what dignity she could muster. ''Would you mind if I asked them up to the house?''

''Don't be ridiculous,'' he shot back through a cloud of smoke. ''I don't play the master around here; the men are always welcome.''

"I didn't mean it that way," she said. She wrapped her arms around her. "Please don't hate me, Egan."

He stood, breathing slowly, deliberately, while his eyes accused. "You knew why I invited you here, Kati," he said after a minute, and his manner was colder than the snow outside. "I didn't make any secret of wanting you. I assumed you felt the same way."

Her eyes lowered to his shirtfront. "I thought I could go through with it," she confessed. "But, last night—" She swallowed. "I was afraid that if I didn't tell you the truth, you'd hurt me."

He made an odd noise deep in his throat and turned away, smoking his cigarette quietly while the clock on the mantel ticked with unnatural loudness.

"I told you once that I like my women experienced. I meant it. I have no taste whatsoever for virgins." He took another harsh draw from the cigarette and moved restlessly around the room, oblivious to her slight flinch. "You're safe for the duration,

Miss James," he said finally, glaring at her. "I wouldn't touch you now to save this ranch."

She would have died before she'd let him see how much that hurt. Her face lifted with what pride she had left. "I won't get in your way," she promised quietly.

"Well, that's comforting," he said sarcastically, and with a smile she didn't like.

Her arms tightened where she had them folded over her breasts. "If that's all, I'd like to have some coffee."

"Help yourself."

She left him, her heart around her ankles. It had been better when she hated him, when she didn't have the memory of his hungry ardor to haunt her. But he'd closed all the doors just now, and there wouldn't be any openings again. He'd as much as said so. Virgins didn't interest him.

She laughed miserably to herself. At least he hadn't guessed that she was in love with him. He hadn't understood that she couldn't have given herself without loving, and that was a blessing. She'd finish her research and get out of there. And once she did, she never wanted to see Egan again. It would be too painful.

For the rest of the day, she went through the motions of living without really feeling much of anything. Dessie noticed, but was kind enough not to say anything.

Finally, faced with imminent insanity or work, Kati chose work. She got out the portable computer and began to write, putting all her frustrations and irritations down on paper in a letter to Egan telling him just what she thought of him. She read it over and then erased every word from the screen without ever having fed it to her printer. She felt much better. Then she began work on the book.

Somehow, writing took all the venom out of her. She created without knowing how she did it, watching the characters unfold on paper, feeling the life-force in them even as she put the words down. When she looked at the clock, she realized that she'd been working for hours. She put the information on tape and then ran it off on the printer for hard copy. After a shower, she went downstairs to see if she could help Dessie with supper.

"No need," Dessie told her with a grin. "We've having beef stew and homemade rolls and a salad. Suit you?"

"Oh, yes! I love beef stew!" she enthused.

"You'll like this—it's our own beef. Want to sit down while I dish it up?"

Kati eased into a chair, noticing that only two places were set. "Just us two?" she asked as casually as she could.

"Boss is helping at the calving sheds. Had a handful of first-time heifers calving tonight, and they've already had to pull one. Gets expensive if you lose too many calves," she explained.

"Is the snow still melting?"

"No, worse luck," Dessie grumbled as she put the food on the table. "Weatherman says it's going to come again tonight. I've seen it so that the snow was over the door."

Kati's heart lodged in her throat. "That high?"

"This is Wyoming," came the laughing reply. "Everything's bigger out West, didn't you know? Now, don't you worry. The boys would dig us out if we got snowed in. And we could get another Chinook."

"I remember a painting by Russell," Kati murmured. "A drawing of a cow freezing in the snow, surrounded by wolves, with the legend 'waiting for a Chinook.' I didn't understand it until now."

"See? You're learning." She nibbled at her stew, watching the younger woman curiously. "Uh, you wouldn't care to tell me a little about this new book? I've read all your others."

Kati's face brightened. "You have?"

"Sure. Well, I know you, sort of." She shifted in the chair. "Gave the girls at the bookstore a charge when I told them that." She glanced up. "I like the books, though, or I wouldn't spend good money on them."

"Just for that," Kati said, "I'll tell you the whole plot."

And Dessie sat, rapt, sighing and smiling, while the entire book was outlined.

"What does the hero look like this time?"
Dessie asked finally. "Is he blond like your
others?"

"No, this one is dark and has silver eyes."

"Like Egan?"

Kati's face flamed red. "His eyes are . . .
gray," she protested.

"Not when he's mad, they ain't. They're
silver, and they gleam." She reached over
and patted the young woman's hand. "Listen, I don't tell Egan nothing. I won't spill
the beans, so don't start clamming up. These
eyes of mine may be old, but they don't miss
a lot. Besides," she added, sipping coffee,
"this morning he ate sausage."

"What does that mean?"

"Egan eats bacon or ham. He hates sausage. I cook it for me." She grinned. "He
wouldn't have noticed if I'd fed him raw
eggs. In a nasty temper, he was."

And Kati knew why, but she wasn't rising
to the bait. "Maybe his tastes have
changed."

"Oh, I know that," Dessie said casually.
"Yes, I do. Have some more stew."

The snow came all night, but Egan didn't appear. It was late the next morning before Kati got a glimpse of him. He came in cursing, stripping off his jacket as he strode toward his study.

"Damned bull," he muttered. "I should have had his horns cut off... Dessie!" he yelled.

She came running, her apron flapping, while Kati stood frozen on the staircase.

"What?" Dessie asked.

"That big Hereford bull of mine got Al," he grumbled. "Get some bandages and disinfectant and I'll drive you down to the bunkhouse to bandage him until I can get the doctor here. I've sent Ramey to fetch him." He jerked up the phone. "Kati!" he called.

She walked in as he was punching buttons. "What can I do?" she asked hesitantly.

"You can stay with Al's wife and keep her quiet," he told her. He held up his hand and spoke into the phone. "Brad, have the boys tracked that wolf yet? Well, call Harry Two

Toes and get him to meet me at the house in twenty minutes. Tell him I'll pay him a thousand dollars for that damned wolf. Right." He hung up the receiver. "Al's wife, Barbara, is pregnant with their first child," he continued, his eyes dark and steady on hers. "I won't let her see him. She gets hysterical at the sight of blood, and she's miscarried twice already. Will you stay with her?"

"Of course," she said without hesitation. "How old is she?"

"Twenty. Just a baby herself. Al was trying to check a sore on that damned bull, and he turned wrong. It's my fault, I should have had him dehorned," he said shortly as he rose from the desk. "Got Al in the stomach. That's a bad place to get gored."

"If he works for you, he must be tough," she said quietly. "He'll be all right, Egan."

His eyes searched hers for a long moment. He turned away. "Get a coat, honey."

She thrilled to the endearment, although she knew that he was worried and probably hadn't realized he was saying it. She ran up the stairs to get her overcoat and knitted hat, and hurried back. Dessie was already wearing a thick corduroy coat of her own, a floppy old hat and hightop boots.

"Let's go," Egan murmured, herding them out into the snow where the truck was parked.

It was slow going. The road was half obscured by the thick, heavy flakes that fell relentlessly. It seemed to take forever to get to the bunkhouse. Egan had Kati wait in the car while he got Dessie inside and checked to see how Al was. He was back minutes later.

"He's stopped bleeding, at least on the outside," he said heavily as he pulled the truck back onto the ruts. "But he's lost color and he's hurting pretty bad. He'll need to go to the hospital, I'm damned sure of that. I told the boys to get him into one of the pickups and put a camper over it and take him into town. I had Ken call Ramey on the radio and have him go on to the hospital instead of to the doctor's and alert the emergency room."

"It's starting out to be a rough day, isn't it?" she asked, thinking of the poor man's wife as well, who still had to be told about the accident.

"Worse." He lit another cigarette. "We had two cows brought down by a wolf and savaged."

"One wolf?" she asked.

"He's old and wily," he told her shortly. "I've lost cows and calves to him for several months now, and I'm at the end of my patience. I'm going to get an Arapaho tracker I know to help me find him."

"You must be losing a lot of money if the wolf is bringing down that many cattle."

"That's not why. I hate killing even a mangy wolf, with the environment in the mess it's in. But you've never seen a cow or a horse that's been attacked by a wolf." His jaws set. "They don't quite kill the animals, you see."

She did, graphically, and her face paled. "Oh."

"We'll trap him and free him in the high country." He turned the truck into the driveway of a small house not far below the bunkhouse.

"Will wolves attack people?" she asked uneasily.

"Not you," he said, half amused. "You won't be walking this ranch alone."

"That's not what I meant." She glanced at him silently.

"Worried about me?" he asked mockingly.

She turned away. "Maybe I was worrying about the wolf," she grumbled.

He got out and helped her over the high bank of snow. She noticed that he didn't offer to carry her this time, and she was glad. It was torture to be close to him, with all the memories between them.

"Try to make her rest as much as you can," Egan said before he knocked on the door. "I'll have Ramey call here just as soon as the doctor's examined Al."

"All right. I'll take care of her."

The door opened, and a pretty young girl with dark hair and eyes opened it. "Egan!"

she said enthusiastically. "What brings you here?"

His eyes went from her swollen belly back to her face and he grimaced. He pulled off his hat. "Barbara, my new Hereford bull gored Al," he said softly. "He's all right, but I've had the boys drive him in to see the doctor."

The girl's face went pale, and Kati stepped forward quickly, as Egan did, to help her back inside and onto a chair.

"I'm Kati," she told the girl as she led her to the chair and eased her bulky figure down into it. "I'm going to stay with you. He'll be all right, Barbara. Egan said so."

Egan looked down at her with a faint smile in his eyes. "I'll be out on the ranch with my tracker," he told Kati. "But if Al isn't home by dark, you'll stay in the house with us, Barbara."

"Yes, Egan," Barbara nodded numbly.

Kati left her long enough to walk out onto the front porch with Egan.

"Keep her as quiet as you can," he said. "If you need help, get Dessie."

"I will," she promised. She looked up at him, quietly searching the craggy lines of his face, loving him so deeply that she'd have followed him barefoot through the snow.

He glanced down at her, and the darkness grew in his eyes as they held hers.

"The wolf," she said uneasily. "You won't take chances?"

He moved close, framing her worried face in his hands, and stared down into her eyes for a long moment. "I never take chances, as a rule," he said. "Of course, I blotted my book with you."

"I don't understand."

"What would you call trying to seduce a virgin on a bearskin rug?" he asked dryly.

She flushed and he laughed.

"I lost my head that night," he told her. "I could have broken your young neck when you told me the truth."

"Yes, I know, and your temper hasn't improved since," she said miserably. "I shouldn't have said anything, I guess."

"I'd have blown my brains out afterward if you hadn't," he said. "Kati, I wasn't in any condition for initiation, ceremonies. You had me so worked up, I didn't know my name. That's why it took me so long to get over it."

"Oh," she murmured, studying him. He didn't look so formidable now. He looked... odd.

"I can't get too close to you, baby, don't you know? I don't want you any less right now than I did the first time I kissed you," he breathed, bending to her mouth. "But I could seduce you now without even trying. And that wouldn't be a good thing."

"It wouldn't?" she whispered, watching his mouth brush and probe gently at hers in the cold air.

"Don't they say," he whispered back, "that good girls almost always get pregnant that first time?"

"Egan...!" she moaned as his mouth found hers.

He lifted her against him and kissed her roughly, his mouth cool and hard and sure as it moved over hers. His gloved hand caught at her nape and brought her face closer; and she heard a deep, rumbling sound echoing out of his chest.

"We've got to stop this," he ground out as his mouth slid across her cheek, and he wrapped her up tightly in his arms. "It's just a matter of time before I go off the deep end if we don't. I could eat you!"

"Yes, I know," she whispered achingly. "I feel the same way."

He rocked her slowly in his arms while the wind whistled around the house and snow blew past them. "I have to go, Kati."

Her arms tightened. "Be careful. Please be careful."

He was breathing heavily, and his eyes when he lifted his head were silvery and wild. "I used to be," he said enigmatically. He let her go and tugged at a lock of her hair with rough affection. "See you, city girl."

She nodded with a weak smile. "So long, cowboy."

She turned and went back into the house before he could see the worried tears in her eyes.

"Would you like some coffee?" she asked Barbara with perfect poise. "If you'll show me where you keep everything, I'll even make it."

Barbara dabbed at her eyes and smiled. "Of course. Thank you for staying with me."

"I'm glad to do what I can for you," Kati replied. "Come on. Your man will be all right. You have to believe that."

"I'm trying to," the young girl replied. She glanced at Kati as they went into the kitchen. "Is Egan your man?"

Kati flushed. "No," she managed. "No, he's my best friend's brother. He's helping me with some research on a book I'm writing."

"You write books?"

"Yes. Those big historical things," Kati offered.

"It must be lots of fun." She got down cups. "I wanted to be a singer, but I married Al instead. We've been together two years now." She stared out the window at the thickening snow. "I love him so much. And we've been so excited about this baby."

"What do you want?" Kati asked, seeing an opening. "A boy or a girl?"

"Oh, a boy," Barbara said. "I've been knitting blue booties and hats. He'll be all right, won't he?"

"Egan said he would, didn't he?" Kati hedged.

Barbara smiled wanly. "I guess so. Egan's never lied."

Kati nodded, but her own mind was on that killer wolf and Egan out hunting it. An animal that would savage cattle three or four times its size would think nothing of attacking a man. She closed her eyes to the possibility. She couldn't bear thinking about it.

Two hours went by before the phone rang, and Kati answered it herself.

"Barbara?" came Ramey's voice.

"No, Ramey, it's Kati. How is Al?" she asked quickly.

"Madder than a skinned snake," Ramey chuckled. "He wants Egan to give him that bull for steaks."

"He's all right!" Kati told Barbara, laughing; and Barbara sat down heavily with a tired sigh.

"The boss might do it, too," Ramey laughed, "despite how much he paid for him. They're going to keep Al overnight, but he wants Barbara with him. Pack her a bag, will you? They're going to put a bed in the room for her."

"I sure will. Are you coming after her?"

"Guess I'll have to. Boss is still out with Charlie."

That was a worrying thought. "Will it take them long to find the wolf, do you think?" she asked hesitantly.

"Anybody's guess, Miss James. See you."

"Bye."

She hung up the phone with numb fingers. "Al wants you to spend the night with him at the hospital. They've even fixed you a bed," she said cheerfully. "He's going to be fine, but Ramey said they want to keep him overnight."

"Oh, thank God, thank God!" Barbara whispered. She took a minute to pull herself together before she became practical. "I'll pack my bag right now. Oh, my poor Al!"

Kati helped her get ready, knowing how she might feel in the same circumstances. And Egan was out tracking that wolf right now. What if something happened to him? How would she manage?

Ramey came and dropped Kati by the house on the way to depositing Barbara at the hospital. Kati waved them off and rushed to find Dessie.

"Is Egan back?" she asked the house-keeper.

Dessie shook her head. "It may take all night. Or longer," she told the obviously worried younger woman. "Kati, he's a rancher. This isn't the first time he's had to go tracking a predator; I doubt if it will be the last. It's something you get used to. Back in the old days," she added with a faint smile, "it was rustlers they chased. And they shot back."

"In other words, the wolf is the lesser of a lot of evils." Kati sighed. "Well..." She

stuck her hands in the pockets of her jeans.
"I guess I'll go work on my book."

"You do that. I'll straighten up the
kitchen. Will you be all right by yourself?
You won't get scared if I go on to bed?"

"Of course not." She was used to Dessie's early hours by now. "I'll just curl up in
a chair and watch TV while I jot down a few
notes. Today has been an education."

"I don't doubt it. Sleep well. Barbara doing okay, was she?"

"Yes. Just worried, and that's natural.
But she handled it well."

"She's a cowboy's wife," Dessie replied.
"Of course she did."

Kati nodded. She was beginning to understand what that meant. She wandered
into the living room and watched television
until bedtime. Still, Egan hadn't come back.

She paced and watched the clock and listened for the sound of a vehicle. But it didn't
come. She thought about going up to bed,
but knew she wouldn't sleep. So she curled
up on the sofa to watch a late-night talk
show. Somewhere in the middle of a star-

let's enthusiasm for designer clothes, she fell asleep.

The dreams were delicious. Someone was holding her, very close; she could feel his breath at her ear, whispering words she couldn't quite hear. She smiled and snuggled close, clinging to a hard neck.

"Did you hear me?"

The sound of Egan's voice brought her awake. Her eyes opened heavily, and she blinked as she saw him above her.

"What time is it?" she asked sleepily.

"Six o'clock in the morning," he said, studying her. He was standing and she was locked close in his arms. She looked around and realized that they were in her bedroom. He'd carried her all the way from the living room and she hadn't known. . . .

"I meant to go to bed," she protested.

"Yes, I imagine you did."

Her eyes searched his drawn face: the growth of beard on his cheeks and chin; the weariness that lay on him like a net. "Did you get the wolf?" she asked softly.

"Yes, honey, we got him." He bent to lay her on the bed and looked straight into her eyes. "Were you waiting up for me, Katriane?"

"No, I was watching television," she protested quickly.

He sat down beside her on the bed, still in his sheepskin coat and the wide-brimmed old hat he wore. He put his fingers over her mouth; they were cold from the outdoors, and he smelled of the wind and fir trees.

"I said," he repeated softly, "were you waiting up for me?"

"Well, you said the stupid creature would attack people, didn't you?"

"I didn't think you'd mind too much if he took a plug out of me," he murmured, studying her sleepy face.

"Isn't that the other way around?" she muttered. "You're the one with all the grudges, not me."

"I wanted you, damn it!" he burst out, glaring at her, and all the controlled anger was spilling out of him. "Wanted you, you naive little idiot! You write about it with a gift, but do you understand what it's like? Men hurt like hell when they get as hot as you got me that night!''

She dropped her eyes to his chest. ''I wasn't going to say no,'' she managed curtly.

''But you knew I would,'' he returned. ''You knew I'd never take you to bed once I had learned the truth. It's not my way.''

''I wasn't thinking,'' she muttered.

''Neither was I. I brought you home thinking I could have you. You knew it. Then, just when I'm involved to the back teeth and aching like a boy of fourteen, you turn it off. Just like that.''

She couldn't bear the accusation in his deep voice, the anger. Her eyes closed and her fingers clenched by her side.

''And the worst part,'' he continued, with barely leashed fury in his tone, ''is that I think you did it deliberately, despite that lame excuse you gave about not wanting me to hurt you. I think you set me up, Kati, to get even.''

That hurt more than all the other accusations put together. It made tears burn her eyes. "What an opinion you have of me," she whispered shakily, trying to force a smile to her lips. "First you think I'm a tramp, and then you try to seduce me, and now you think I'm a cheat besides."

"Don't try to throw it back on my head!" he growled.

"Why not?" She sat up, glaring. "Why not? You were the one who kept putting on the pressure, weren't you? And every time I tried to explain, you shut me up!"

"You knew why I invited you," he shot back. "For God's sake, what did you come out here expecting, a proposal of marriage!"

That was so close to the truth that it took all her control not to let him see it. "Of course not," she replied instead, as coolly as she could. "I expected to be allowed to research my book. And you told me," she added levelly, "that there were no strings attached. Didn't you?"

He sighed angrily but he didn't deny it. His eyes searched over her flushed, angry face, her narrowed eyes. "I guess I did."

Her breasts rose and fell softly, and she looked down at her hands. "As soon as the snow melts a little, I'll leave. I'll need some more data on Wyoming history and a few other related subjects, but I can get that in Cheyenne."

"Writing is all that matters to you, isn't it?" he asked coldly.

She met his eyes. "Egan, what else do I have?"

His heavy brows drew together. "You're young."

"I'll see my twenty-sixth summer this year," she replied. "And all I have to show for my life is a few volumes of historical fiction in the 'J' section of the library. No family. No children. No nothing."

"I'm almost thirty-five and in the same predicament, and I don't give a damn," he told her.

She studied his hard face. "I'm not even surprised. You don't need anyone."

"I do need the occasional woman," he replied.

"I'm sorry, but I don't do occasionals," she told him. "I'm the forever-after type, and if you'd really read any of my books, you'd have known it before you ruined everything."

"I ruined everything?" He glared at her thunderously. "You couldn't get your clothes off fast enough!"

"Oh!" Shamed to the bones, she felt the tears come, and she hated her own weakness. She tried to get up, but he caught her, his hands steely on her upper arms.

"I didn't mean to say that," he ground out. "Damn you, Kati, you bring out everything mean and ornery in my soul!"

"Then it's a good thing I'm leaving before you just rot away, isn't it?" she said, weeping.

He drew in a deep, slow breath. "Oh baby," he breathed, drawing her close against him under the unbuttoned sheepskin coat. "Baby, I don't want to hurt you."

His voice was oddly tender, although she barely heard the words through her sobs.

She'd hardly cried in her life until Egan came along.

His arms enclosed her warmly and she felt his cold, rough cheek against hers as he held her. "You've had a hard time of it, haven't you? I wouldn't have asked you to stay with Barbara, but I needed Dessie more to get Al patched."

"I didn't mind, truly I didn't. She was so brave."

"She's had to be. Living out here isn't easy on a woman. It's still hard country, and winters can be terrifying. Spring comes and there's flooding. Summer may bring a drought. A man can lose everything overnight out here." He stroked her hair absently. "It was even harder on Barbara. She was a California girl."

"She loves him, Egan."

He laughed shortly, the sound echoing heavily in the dark room. "And love is enough?"

"You make it sound sordid," she murmured at his ear, stirring slightly.

"Well, women set great store by it, I suppose," he said quietly. "I never did. What passed for love in my life was bought and paid for."

She flinched at the cynicism and drew back to look at him. This close, she could see every line in that craggy face. It held her eyes like a magnet, from the kindling silver eyes to the square chin that badly needed a razor.

"Haven't you ever loved anyone?" she asked gently.

"My mother. Ada."

"A lover," she persisted, searching his eyes.

"No, Katriane," he told her somberly. "The few times I tried, I found out pretty quick that it was the money they wanted, not me. What was it you called me that last time we got into it— a big, ugly cowboy?"

"I meant it, too," she said, not backing down. "But what I was talking about had nothing to do with looks. No, Egan, you aren't at all handsome. But you're all man, so what difference does it make?"

He stared at her, and she flushed, averting her eyes. She hadn't meant to let that slip out.

His fingers toyed with her hair and worked their way under her chin to lift it. He was closer than she'd expected—so close that all she could see was his nose and mouth.

"It's been...a long time since anyone waited up for me. Or worried over me," he said huskily. His breath came heavily. "Kati, you'd better not let me have your mouth."

But she wanted it. Ached for it. And her eyes told him so. He caught his breath at the blatant hunger in them.

"I'll hurt you," he ground out.

"I don't even care...!" She reached up, opening her arms and her heart, and dragged his open, burning mouth down onto hers.

He was rough. Not only in the crushing hold he had on her slender body, but the bristly pressure of his face and the ardent hunger of his mouth. His fingers tangled in her long hair and twirled it around and around, arching her neck.

His lips lifted, poised over hers, and he was breathing as raggedly as she was. "Open your mouth a little more," he said shakily. "Let me show you how I like to be kissed."

Her eyes opened so that she could look into his, and his hands clasped the back of her head as he ground his mouth into hers again, feeling it open and tremble and want his.

"Kati," he breathed as he half lifted her against him, while the kiss became something out of her experience. "God, Kati, it's so sweet . . . !"

She clung to him, giving back the ardent pressure until he groaned and his rough cheek slid against hers and he held her, breathing in shudders at her ear.

"Stop letting me do that," he ground out, tightening his arms. "It only makes things worse!"

"Yes," she whispered shakily. Her face nuzzled against his, her eyes closed, her body aching for something it had never had.

She began to realize what was happening to him, and it was her fault. She sat perfectly still in his arms and let him hold her until his breathing was steady, until the slight tremor went out of his arms.

"I'm sorry," she whispered.

"Yes, I know, but it doesn't help," he murmured.

"Well, don't put all the blame on me!" she sobbed, trying to push him away.

"I'm not trying to. Stop fighting me."

"Stop making horrible remarks."

He laughed. Laughed! He rubbed his face against hers affectionately; it felt like a pincushion. He lifted his head, and his eyes were blazing with laughter and something much harder to identify. He looked down at her, searching her eyes, her face, and looking so utterly smug that she wanted to hit him.

"You are something else," he said, and she remembered the words from the night he'd made love to her by the fire. She blushed scarlet, and he lifted an eyebrow. "Remembering, are you?" His eyes went down to her blouse and stayed there. "I'll never forget."

Her eyes closed because she couldn't bear the heat of his gaze. "Neither will I. I never meant—"

"Don't," he whispered, bringing her close again. "We made magic that night. I had this opinion of you, you see. For a long time. Kati, I wasn't telling the truth when I said I'd read your books, I'd only read a passage or two. Just enough to support my negative assessment of your character." He lifted his head and looked down at her. "Night before last, I read one. Really read it. There are some pretty noticeable gaps in those love scenes." He searched her eyes. "But some pretty powerful emotions in them, all the same. They were beautiful."

Her eyes burned with tears. "Thank you."

He touched her cheek softly. "I'd like very much to make love with you that way, Kati," he whispered. "I'd like to lie with you on a deserted beach in the moonlight and watch your body move, the way that pirate did in your last book...."

"Don't," she pleaded, burying her face in his shirt. She didn't feel at all like the very cool author who spoke to writers' clubs with such poise. She felt . . . young.

"So shy with me," he whispered, lifting her across his lap. "And I was the first, wasn't I? The first man to look at you, to touch you, to be intimate with you. My God, I ache just thinking about it, when it never mattered a damn before how many men I'd followed with a woman." His hands smoothed over her back gently while his face nuzzled hers. "I'm like a boy with you, Kati. When we share those deep, hot kisses, I shake all over."

Her fingers made patterns on his shirt, and she loved the bigness and warmth of his body so close to hers. But he was admitting to nothing except desire. And she wanted much, much more.

"We'd better go and eat, I suppose," he murmured. "And I need a shave and a bath." He lifted his head and studied her pink cheek where his had scraped it, and he smiled slowly. "If we made love and I hadn't shaved, you'd look like that all over," he commented.

It brought to mind pictures that made her ache, and she couldn't get away from him quickly enough.

"There's just one thing," he added, watching her with a lazy smile. "If I ever turn up in one of those damned books, you're in trouble."

"I don't write about real people," she defended, and prayed that he'd never see the first few chapters of her new book before she had time to turn the hero back into a blond.

"You'd better not," he said; and although his voice was pleasant, there was a hard glint in his eyes. "What we do together when we make love is private. For the two of us alone."

She frowned. "You can't believe I'd do that!"

He searched her eyes slowly. "I'm not a writer. Explain it to me."

"It would take hours," she told him.

"I'm not leaving for the rest of the day," he told her. "Let me get my bath and shave. I'll meet you downstairs. You can ask me anything else you need to know about the ranch while we're at it."

The prospect of spending a day alone with him was heady and sweet. "All right," she said.

He winked and went out the door, already a different man. For the rest of the day, they talked as never before. He told her about the early days of the ranch and how his grandfather came by it. He told her about his own plans for it; his dreams; the career he once thought he wanted in politics. In return, she explained to him how she felt her characters come alive on paper and take over the actual writing of the book, right down to the love scenes. She explained how she researched the historical facts and how she'd learned to grit her teeth and smile when people asked where she had learned so much about intimacy when she was unmarried and apparently living alone.

"You see, it's just that you can't write fiction without a little romance." She sighed. "And these days, the more sensuous the better. I won't go the whole hog and write explicit scenes, but the sexiest books are the biggest sellers. I must be pretty accurate, though, because my reader mail is mostly kind.''

He shook his head, sitting quietly by the crackling fireplace, watching her. ''A virgin. Writing what you write. My God.''

''Well, most fiction about scientists isn't written by scientists. Most fiction about lawyers isn't written by lawyers. It's just a matter of research, like anything else,'' she added.

''You do it very—''

The telephone interrupted him. Expecting news about Al, he sprang to his feet to answer.

''Hello?'' His face changed. ''Yes, how are you, Jennie?''

Kati felt her body go rigid. That woman! So they did have something going, even after he'd left New York.

''Yes, I know.'' He toyed with a pen-set on the desk. ''Umm-hmm. Yes, we did, didn't we?'' He smiled. ''Here? No, I don't think that's a good idea, honey. We're snowed in. That's right, about five feet of it. No, we've closed the landing strip. You'd have to fly in to Jackson. Maybe. Tell you what, let's put it off until spring. Yes, I know you don't, but that's how it is, Jennie. No strings, remember? I told you at the very beginning how it was going to be. That's right. Sure. Next time I'm in town. So long." He hung up and turned, watching the expressions cross Kati's face.

"She wanted to stop over for a week or two on her way to California for a screen test," he volunteered. "I said no. Anything else you'd like to know?"

"She . . . was very pretty," Kati muttered.

"Surely she was. And experienced," he added deliberately. "But she wanted ties and I didn't."

"Freedom is your big problem, isn't it?" she asked on a laugh. "Well, don't look at me as if I had a rope in one hand—I don't want strings any more than you do," she lied, and looked away just in time to miss the expression that froze his face.

"I thought all you women wanted marriage," he said in an odd voice.

"Not now I don't," she returned as casually as she could. "I'm too involved in work."

"Going to remain a virgin for life, I gather?" he asked cuttingly. "Give up a home and children so you can keep writing those damned books?"

She looked up with a deliberate smile, in spite of the glittering anger in his eyes. "I like writing those damned books."

He turned away. "So I noticed. Don't let me hold you up, you probably have a lot of work to get through if you're leaving by the end of the week."

And he walked out of the room, leaving her speechless. Well, what had he expected her to say, she wondered achingly—that she loved him? That she'd lie on the floor and let him walk on her if she could stay with him?

Fat chance! If he could brush Jennie off so easily, when he'd obviously had an affair with her, what chance did she have? Probably he was just biding his time until he could get her into his bed. He knew she'd surrender, she thought miserably, he knew very well that she couldn't resist him. And once she'd given in, he'd be letting her down easily, just the way he'd done Jennie. And he'd be in pursuit of some new woman. With a tiny moan, she went upstairs and opened the case that held her computer. What a miserable end for a wonderful day!

Chapter Eleven

It wasn't hard to avoid Egan after that. He wasn't home. He worked from dawn until late at night and appeared only briefly to eat. He treated Kati with grudging courtesy, but he didn't come near her.

She packed Friday morning to go back to New York. The snow was melting again, and the skies were sunny and clear. Perhaps, she told herself, it was an omen.

"I sure am going to miss you," Dessie said gruffly as she had breakfast with Kati and

Egan. "Been nice, having another woman around the place."

"I'll miss you, too," Kati said genuinely as she finished her eggs and drank her coffee. "I've learned a lot while I was here."

"I reckon Gig's talked more in the past week than he has since I've known him," Egan said mockingly. He leaned back precariously in his cane-bottom chair to study her as he smoked a cigarette. He seemed to smoke all the time these days. "Have you satisfied your curiosity about ranch life, Miss Author?" he added.

"Yes," she said, refusing to let him irritate her. "And about the cattle business. Thank you for letting me come."

"My pleasure. Any time." He swallowed the rest of his coffee and got to his feet. "Ramey's going to drive you to the airport."

"Ramey?" Dessie burst out. "But Egan, you never let Ramey— "

"Just never mind, if you please," he told the old woman, a bite in his voice. He glanced at Kati hard, and his eyes accused.

"I'll clear this stuff away," Dessie murmured quickly and retreated into the kitchen with two empty platters.

"Have a safe trip home," he told Kati quietly. "And give Ada my love."

"I'll do that," she said stiffly.

He started to pass by her, paused, and suddenly jerked her out of the chair by her arms, hurting her as he dragged her against his chest.

"Damn you," he breathed furiously, with silver eyes that glittered dangerously. "Do you think your career is going to keep you warm at night? Will it give you what I did on that bearskin rug by the fireplace?" he demanded.

Her body melted against his and she wished she had the strength to hit him, but she was drowning in his eyes and the feel of his taut, powerful body.

"What are you offering me?" she asked. "A night in your bed?"

His hands tightened on her arms and he looked hunted. "I don't want you to leave," he said gruffly. "We'll work it out some-how."

"How?" she persisted. "Egan, I'm not like Jennie. I can't take an open affair."

"What do you want, then?" he asked under his breath, watching her. "Marriage?"

She searched his angry eyes defeatedly. "You'd hate me for that," she said with quiet perception.

"I don't know," he replied. "We might get used to each other; make a go of it."

She reached up, touching his face softly with her fingertips. "You'd better stick to girls like Jennie," she said softly. "I couldn't settle for what you'd be able to give me. I couldn't live on crumbs."

"I'm a rich man," he said curtly. "You could have anything you wanted, within reason. And in bed, I'd be everything you'd ever need."

"I know that," she agreed. Her fingers traced his hard mouth, feeling its automatic response with wonder. "But it's still not enough."

"Why not, for God's sake?" he growled, catching her wandering fingers roughly in his own.

"Because I'm in love with you, Egan," she said proudly, watching the reaction flare in his eyes, harden his face. "You can't match that with money or sex. I'd wither away and die of neglect and pity. No, I'd rather be totally alone than on my knees at your heart."

His lips parted and he couldn't seem to find the right words. He touched her hair hesitantly. "You love me?" he whispered huskily, frowning as if he found the words incomprehensible.

"Occupational hazard," she whispered, trying not to cry. "I'll get over it. Good-bye, Egan."

His fingers tightened in her hair. "No, not yet," he said uncertainly. "Not just yet. You don't have to go right now—"

"Yes, I do," she said, on the verge of tears. "I'm running out of pride—" Her voice broke, and she tried to get away, but his arms tightened like a vice and he held her despite her struggles.

"Don't," he whispered, shaken. "Don't fight me. My God, Kati, don't run."

"Egan," she moaned.

"Egan!" Dessie called sharply from the kitchen. "It's the hospital on the phone! Something about Al— Can you come?"

He cursed under his breath, looking down at the tears on Kati's cheeks with eyes that frightened her. "Don't move," he said shortly. "Not one step. You hear me?"

She nodded, but the minute he was out of sight, she grabbed up her bag and made a run for the front door. She couldn't face him again, not after the fool she'd made of herself. If she couldn't have his love, she didn't want his pity. She couldn't bear it!

As luck would have it, Ramey was just getting out of the pickup truck. She dived in on the passenger side.

"Ramey, can you get me to the airport in Jackson in a hurry?" she asked quickly. "There's an emergency—I have to leave!"

"Emergency?" Ramey jumped back in and started the truck. "Why sure, Miss James. Don't you worry, I'll get you there!"

He turned the truck, and Kati reached down and very unobtrusively cut off the two-way radio.

"That noise is just awful," she murmured, "and I have such a headache. Can't we leave it off just until we get to town?" she asked with a pitiful smile.

He hesitated, then he grinned. "Sure. I don't reckon we'll need it."

"Good!" And then she began to talk furiously to keep his mind occupied. It didn't hurt her, either, to stop thinking about Egan and the look on his face when she'd confessed. She didn't know if she'd be able to hear his name again without going mad.

It seemed to take forever, and despite the four-wheel drive and snow tires, they almost bogged down a few times. But Ramey got her to the airport. It wasn't until she was getting out that she realized she'd left her computer at the ranch.

"I'll tell the Boss," Ramey assured her. "He'll get it to you."

That wasn't a comforting thought; the Boss would be out for blood. But she smiled anyway. "Thanks." She'd just do those chapters over on her stationary computer at the apartment, she assured herself; she could remember most of them.

"Have a good trip!" Ramey called and was off with a wave of his hand.

There was a seat on an outgoing plane to Cheyenne. She'd hole up there for a few days, letting only Ada know where she was. She wasn't strong enough to resist Egan, so she wasn't going to try.

She kept watching the door, although she couldn't help wondering why. Egan wouldn't come after her. Besides, she thought, he'd never make it through the snow anyway.

She checked her bag, went aboard with only her purse, and sat down heavily in her seat. It was over. She was leaving. Now all she had to do was get her mind off Egan and find some way of not thinking about him for the rest of her life. Facing Ada was going to

be hard. Living with her would be sheer torture. She knew she'd die every time Ada
mentioned her brother.

The plane was running now, and she knew
it wouldn't be long until takeoff. She was
just starting to fasten her seat belt when she
heard a commotion in the back of the plane.

A sheepskin coat came suddenly into view,
with a hard, furious face above it.

While she was getting over the shock,
Egan reached down, unfastened her seat belt
and scooped her up in his hard arms, purse
and all.

"You can't do this!" she burst out, oblivious to the amused eyes of the other passen-
gers.

"Like hell I can't," he replied curtly and
carried her off the plane.

"Oh Egan, let me go!" she wailed as he
walked back toward the terminal, burying
her embarrassed face in his warm collar.

"I can't," he whispered huskily, and his
arms tightened around her.

Tears rolled down her cheeks. He wanted
her, that was all, but she didn't have the

strength to walk away again, even if he'd let her. So she lay in his arms, crying softly, and let him carry her all the way to his pickup truck.

He put her in and got in beside her, picking up the radio mike as he started the truck. He gave his call letters and told somebody he was on his way back with Kati and signed off.

"My bag," she began.

"I hope it has a nice trip," he said curtly, glaring at her as he pulled out into the road. "I told you to stay put."

"I couldn't," she muttered miserably, staring into her lap. "I was too embarrassed."

"Best-selling author," he scoffed, glaring toward her. "The sensual mistress of the ages. And you can't tell a man you love him without blushing all over?"

"I've never done it before!" she burst out, glaring back at him.

His silver eyes gleamed. "You're doing a lot of firsts with me, aren't you, city girl? And the biggest and best is still to come."

"I won't sleep with you, Egan," she said angrily.

"Won't you?" He lit a cigarette and smoked it with a smile so arrogant she wanted to hit him.

"I want to go home!"

"You are home, honey," he replied. "Because that's what White Lodge is going to be from now on."

"Do be reasonable," she pleaded, turning toward him. "You're asking me to give up everything I believe in!"

"That's where you're wrong, Kati. I'm not asking."

"I'll scream," she threatened.

He gave her a wicked smile. "Yes, you probably will," he murmured softly.

"Oh, damn," she wailed.

"Now just calm down, honey," he told her. "When we get back to the ranch, I'll explain it all to you. Right now, you'd better let me keep my mind on the road. I don't want to spend the rest of the day sitting in a ditch."

She sighed. "How's Al?" she asked dully, remembering the phone call.

"On his way home. He called to get one of the boys to drive him. Now hush."

She folded her arms across her chest, feeling miserable and cold and helpless. He was taking the choice away from her, and she didn't know what to do. Didn't he realize what he was forcing on her? She wouldn't be able to go on living afterward, because the memory of him would burn into her like a brand and she'd never be free again. How could he be so cruel?

It seemed to take much less time getting back to White Lodge than it had leaving it. Egan pulled up at the steps and cut off the engine.

"I won't go in," she muttered.

"I figured you were going to be unpleasant about it," he said on a sigh. He got out, lifted her from the cab of the truck and carried her into the house.

"Dessie, take the phone off the hook," he told the amused housekeeper. "I've got a lot of explaining to do, and I don't want to be interrupted.''

''Just keep in mind I'll be out here with my frying pan,'' Dessie told him, winking at Kati. ''And keeping the coffee hot.''

He laughed under his breath, carrying Kati into his study. He slammed the door behind him and put her down so that he could lock it.

She retreated to the fireplace, where a fire was crackling merrily, and glanced down at the bearskin rug. She quickly moved away, and Egan watched her as he took off his hat and coat, his eyes sparkling with amusement.

''It wasn't that bad, was it?'' he asked, nodding toward the rug. ''I thought you enjoyed what I did to you on that.''

''Don't you have work to do?'' she asked, moving behind his desk.

''Afraid of me, Kati?'' he asked softly, moving toward her.

He looked devastating. All lean grace and muscle. His dark hair was mussed, and his eyes were sensual.

"Egan, let me go to New York," she said unsteadily, backing up until the wall stopped her.

He moved toward her relentlessly, until she was trapped between the hard wall and his taut body. He put his hands deliberately beside her head, the way he had in the kitchen that morning, and she trembled with the hunger to feel that hard body crushing down on hers.

"Now we talk," he said softly, watching the emotions play on her face. "You told me you loved me. How? Is it just a physical thing, or is it more?"

Her lips parted on a rush of breath and her body ached for him. He poised there, taunting her; and, involuntarily, she moved against the wall.

"Tell me," he whispered, "and I'll do what you want me to do."

She swallowed, so weak with love that she couldn't even protest that arrogance. "I love you in every way there is," she told him. "Every single way."

"I've got a nasty temper," he reminded her quietly. "I like my own way. And I've lived alone for a long time. It won't be easy. There are going to be times when you'll wish I hadn't carried you off that plane."

Her body felt like jelly as she looked up at him. "I love you," she whispered. "I love you!"

He eased down over her, letting her feel the full, devastating effect the words had on him, and he smiled at the mingled hunger and embarrassment in her face.

"I'll want a son," he murmured, watching the effect of that soft statement. "Maybe three or four of them."

She smiled slowly, wonderingly. "I'd like that, too," she said, trembling as she realized what he was saying.

"No big wedding, though," he added under his breath as his body began to move slowly, sensuously, against hers. "Just the minister and some of the boys and Ada."

"Yes," she whispered, lifting her mouth, pleading for his.

"And if a word of what I'm about to do to you gets into print," he threatened with his mouth poised just above hers, "I'll chase you to Jackson with the truck."

"Yes, darling," she whispered back, standing on tiptoe to reach his open mouth with hers. "Egan, what are you going to do to me?"

"Come here and I'll tell you," he murmured on a soft laugh.

She felt his fingers taking away the sweater and opening the blouse, but she was too busy unbuttoning his shirt to care. Seconds later, hard, hair-roughened muscle pressed against soft, bare breasts; and she moaned, lifting her arms around his neck as she moved hungrily under him.

"Not here," he groaned. He lifted her and carried her to the rug, easing her down onto it.

"You can't imagine," she managed shakily as he lifted himself over her trembling body, "how many books I've read this scene in."

"You can't imagine," he countered, "how different this is going to be from reading." His hands slid under her, lifting her to the hard pressure of his hips, and he watched her with glittering silver eyes as she cried out. "You see?" he whispered unsteadily. "Kati, I'm drowning in you. Drowning in the feel of you, the taste of you."

He bent, and she gave him her mouth totally, moving instinctively under the weight of his taut body, loving the heaviness and hunger that was crushing her in pleasure.

"Like this," he whispered, guiding, and she felt him in a new and shocking way, and her eyes flew open incredulously.

His face, above hers, was hard with desire, his eyes glittering with triumph as he saw her pleasure in her eyes. "Now," he breathed, and his hands went under her thighs. "Now, just do what I tell you."

She felt his mouth on hers through a fog of incredible hunger, and somewhere in the middle of it, she began to cry. It was the sweetest maelstrom in the world. She felt the rough silk of his skin under her hands, and she touched him in ways she'd never dreamed of touching a man. Her legs tangled with his while he taught her sensations that shocked and burned and stung with pleasure.

"Please, Egan," she whispered into his ear, gasping as he lifted her hips closer. "Please, please!"

"I want you just as much," he whispered back. "But we're not going all the way."

"Egan!" she groaned.

"Trust me, Kati," he whispered. "Give me your mouth, and lie still."

She did, and somewhere in the back of her mind she felt as if she were dying as his body stilled on hers and his mouth began to lose its obsession with hers. He stroked her and whispered to her, and she cried helplessly as the urgency began to recede, to calm into a pleasant exhaustion.

"You and I," he whispered, "are going to burn up when we make love for the first time. I've never felt in my life what I feel when you put your hands on me."

She smoothed his dark hair with fingers that still trembled, and nuzzled against the hair over his hard chest. "Will it be enough?"

His lips brushed over her closed eyelids. "Look at me, little virgin," he whispered. "I want to watch your eyes when I say it."

Her heavy eyelids lifted and she saw his eyes burn like sunlight.

"I love you, Kati," he whispered softly. "I loved you the night you came walking home with my cousin, and I was so eaten up with jealousy that I ate you alive. I've loved you every day since and fought it with everything in me."

Her lips parted but she couldn't speak. Oh God, it was like having every dream of love she'd ever dreamed come true all at once!

"I thought you were having a fling," he said tightly. "Until the night we lay here together and you told me the truth. And I wanted to go through the floor, because I'd misread the whole situation, and I'd said things to you that still make me uneasy." He brushed the hair away from her cheeks and

let his gaze drift down to her soft bareness.
His jaw clenched and he dragged his eyes
back up to hers, while his fingers stroked
over skin no man had touched before.
"Then you said you didn't want ties, and I
realized that I did. I wanted my ring on your
finger, for all time. But you were leaving.
And I couldn't find the right words." He
sighed heavily. "I was trying to, when you
told me you loved me."

"I thought I'd embarrassed you," she said
softly.

"You'd given me the moon, Kati," he replied, watching her. "The moon, the sun,
the stars—I was speechless, just savoring the
feel of it, the sound. And then Al called, and
you got away. I'd have gone down on my
knees to you . . . !"

"Egan," she breathed, drawing him close
with possessive arms, clinging passionately
to him. "Egan, it tore me apart to go! But I
was afraid you'd pity me."

"I pitied myself for being so damned stupid—for ever letting you out of my sight. It
will be the last time, too. As soon as I get a

license, we're getting married. Tomorrow, if possible.''

"But, I don't have a dress!''

"Get married in blue jeans, for all I care,'' he told her. "I just want to give you my name. My heart. My life.''

Her eyes closed on a wave of pleasure. Tears welled up in them, at the magnificence of loving and being loved in return. She shuddered.

"Cold?'' he whispered, concerned. "I'd forgotten how little we have on.''

She did blush then, as he handed her her blouse and bra and watched her struggle to rearrange her jeans.

"Don't stare,'' she pleaded.

"I can't help it. You're so lovely,'' he said with a grin. He propped himself on an elbow, devastating without his shirt. "I guess we'll have to have at least one daughter to look like you.'' He caught her hand when she finished buttoning buttons and clasped it warmly to his hard, furry chest. "Can you live here with me and not miss the excitement of the city?''

"My darling," she said softly, "I carry my excitement around in my imagination, and I can work on the roof if I have to. There's a post office in Jackson. I have you to keep me warm and love me. What else do I need?"

He smiled slowly. "A good supply of sexy nightgowns," he murmured.

"Now, in that last book I wrote," she whispered, easing down beside him, "the heroine had this very modest white gown..."

"Which the hero ripped off on page fifty-six," he chuckled softly. "Yes, I know, but I like that scene in the bathtub. So, suppose tomorrow night you and I try it out?"

"I thought you were afraid of my research turning up in books," she laughed.

"Not since I've been reading them," he replied. "Anyway, they're giving me some good ideas."

She lifted her arms around his neck and pulled him down. "Suppose we just work on this bearskin-rug scene a little more?" she whispered at his lips. "I don't think I've got it the way I want it just yet."

"After we're married," he whispered back, his voice husky with emotion as he stared into her eyes, "we'll lie here together and go all the way. I'll let you feel this rug under you while I lie over you and—"

"Egan," she groaned, trembling, hiding her face.

He laughed softly as he pressed her back into it. "I can see that having a virgin for a wife is going to be educational," he mused.

"It's sort of the other way around right now, though," she reminded him. "You're the one doing the teaching."

"So I am." He rubbed his nose against hers. "And I'll tell you a secret, city girl. It's a hell of a lot more fun than fighting."

She smiled. Indeed it was, she thought as his lips nuzzled against hers. She caressed his back lovingly, and she wondered if Ada was going to be surprised when they called her. Somehow, she didn't think so. She reached up and pulled Egan's head down to hers. Outside, the snow began to fall softly, again.

* * * * *

WESTERN *Lovers*

AVAILABLE IN JANUARY

Another
Western Lovers
ready to rope and tie your heart!

HEART OF ICE—
Diana Palmer
Denim & Diamonds

The last thing city girl Kati James wanted to do
was spend Christmas with an arrogant, rugged
Wyoming rancher. But once Egan Winthrop got
Kati under the mistletoe, he never intended to let
her go...

HARLEQUIN® *Silhouette*®

WL196

Take 4 bestselling love stories FREE

Plus get a FREE surprise gift!

Special Limited-time Offer

Mail to Silhouette Reader Service™

3010 Walden Avenue
P.O. Box 1867
Buffalo, N.Y. 14269-1867

YES! Please send me 4 free Silhouette Romance™ novels and my free surprise gift. Then send me 6 brand-new novels every month, which I will receive months before they appear in bookstores. Bill me at the low price of $2.44 each plus 25¢ delivery and applicable sales tax, if any.* That's the complete price and a savings of over 10% off the cover prices—quite a bargain! I understand that accepting the books and gift places me under no obligation ever to buy any books. I can always return a shipment and cancel at any time. Even if I never buy another book from Silhouette, the 4 free books and the surprise gift are mine to keep forever.

215 BPA AW6X

Name	(PLEASE PRINT)	
Address	Apt. No.	
City	State	Zip

This offer is limited to one order per household and not valid to present Silhouette Romance™ subscribers. *Terms and prices are subject to change without notice. Sales tax applicable in N.Y.

USROM-995   ©1990 Harlequin Enterprises Limited

Are your lips
succulent, impetuous,
delicious or racy?

Find out in a very special Valentine's Day
promotion—THAT SPECIAL KISS!

Inside four special Harlequin and Silhouette February
books are details for THAT SPECIAL KISS!
explaining how you can have your lip prints read
by a romance expert.

Look for details in the following series books,
written by four of Harlequin and Silhouette readers'
favorite authors:

Silhouette Intimate Moments #691
Mackenzie's Pleasure by *New York Times*
bestselling author Linda Howard

Harlequin Romance #3395
Because of the Baby by Debbie Macomber

Silhouette Desire #979
Megan's Marriage by Annette Broadrick

Harlequin Presents #1793
The One and Only by Carole Mortimer

Fun, romance, four top-selling authors, plus a **FREE**
gift! This is a very special Valentine's Day you won't
want to miss! Only from Harlequin and Silhouette.

HARLEQUIN® **Silhouette®**

VAL96

Bestselling author

RACHEL LEE

takes her Conard County series to new heights with

A CONARD COUNTY *Reckoning*

This March, Rachel Lee brings readers a brand-new, longer-length, out-of-series title featuring the characters from her successful Conard County miniseries.

Janet Tate and Abel Pierce have both been betrayed and carry deep, bitter memories. Brought together by great passion, they must learn to trust again.

"Conard County is a wonderful place to visit! Rachel Lee has crafted warm, enchanting stories. These are wonderful books to curl up with and read. I highly recommend them."
—*New York Times* bestselling author
Heather Graham Pozzessere

Available in March, wherever Silhouette books are sold.

You're About to Become a *Privileged Woman*

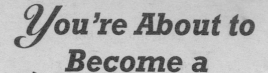

Reap the rewards of fabulous free gifts and benefits with proofs-of-purchase from Harlequin and Silhouette books

Pages & Privileges™

It's our way of thanking you for buying our books at your favorite retail stores.

**Harlequin and Silhouette—
the most privileged readers in the world!**

For more information about Harlequin and Silhouette's PAGES & PRIVILEGES program call the Pages & Privileges Benefits Desk: 1-503-794-2499

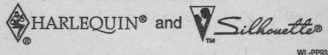

HARLEQUIN® and Silhouette®

WL-PP93